'The bristling, dark humour of [Rhodes'] first collection was still very much in evidence as he continued to describe the desperate lengths the human heart is driven to in attempting to fulfill its desires.'   *Waterstone's Books Quarterly*

'Underneath the quirky surface, this is a book as dark as any and Rhodes' writing, full of black humour, comes crashing through.'

                              Big Issue Scotland

Praise for *Timoleon Vieta Come Home*
and Dan Rhodes

'The delightful story of a lost dog, his bereft owner
and a heartless interloper.' *Guardian*

'It is funny, beguiling and sentimental, with a dark
undertow that will tug at the memory.'

Time Magazine

'*Timoleon Vieta Come Home* takes a broader view
of the theme of disappointed love, exploring with
a beguiling mix of humour and poignancy the
many ways in which love is given, betrayed or
lost – between lovers, between parent and child,
even between a man and man's best friend.'

Bookseller

'Highly original.' *Vogue*

'Rhodes has written a book which has sentiment
without schmaltz, humanity with a cynical edge . . .
Timoleon Vieta hits home.' *Big Issue in the North*

'This book is remarkably moving.'

Sunday Tribune

'Much of *Timoleon Vieta* is crude and much of it is cruel. But Rhodes is a writer unafraid to empathise with the failed and the eccentric. He is an imperfect but undeniably entertaining author.'

Sunday Herald

'Dan Rhodes has a marvellous ear for the comically absurd.' *Red Magazine*

'Both gripping and imaginative, this is one of those books you will come back to read time and again.' *What's On in London*

'Rhodes' style is wonderfully efficient and economic throughout, but he can evoke whole lives and histories in just a few precise sentences, making this an unusual but wonderful and moving work.' *The List (Scotland)*

TIMOLEON VIETA COME HOME

A Sentimental Journey

Dan Rhodes

CANONGATE

First published in the UK in 2003 by
Canongate Books Ltd, 14 High Street, Edinburgh
EH1 1TE

This edition published in 2004

3

Copyright © Dan Rhodes, 2003
The moral rights of the author have been asserted

British Library Cataloguing-in-Publication Data
A catalogue record for this book is available on request
from the British Library

ISBN 1 84195 481 0

Typeset by Palimpsest Book Production Limited,
Polmont, Stirlingshire
Printed and bound by Clays Ltd, St Ives plc

www.canongate.net

ACKNOWLEDGEMENTS

Many thanks to Christopher Meredith (my Cymraeg consultant), Sheenagh Pugh (for services above and beyond), Sairah Woods (likewise), Jamie, Stan and Colin and all my other saviours at Canongate, my many allies during the Summer, Autumn and Winter of Discontent (who I am far too discreet to name – thank you all), the Society of Authors, WB & VC Rhodes and, of course, Blimey.

Special thanks to Vien Thuc for allowing me to use his paintings of dogs. His extraordinary gallery can be found at Lam Ty Ni Pagoda, 2 Duong Thien My, Da Lat, Lam Dong, Vietnam.

CONTENTS

PART ONE: TIMOLEON VIETA

PART TWO: TIMOLEON VIETA COME HOME

. . .dogs are owned by men, and men are bludgeoned by fate.

From *Lassie Come-Home* by Eric Knight.

PART ONE

Timoleon Vieta

TIMOLEON VIETA

Timoleon Vieta was the finest breed of dog. He was a mongrel.

The self-conscious preening, superior airs and inbred neuroses of the pedigree were not for him. His heritage was clearly such a mess that any attempt to untangle it could only be a futile exercise. Even so, its very mystery had served to revive a few flagging conversations as people scrutinised him and saw beauceron in his coat, a touch of Swedish Vallhund in his outsized ears, something Nordic in the slight curl of his tail, pinscher in his gait, or sloth in the way he so often lay on the ground or in the armchair he had made his own. But really there was nothing much to go on, and nothing pure to save.

Nobody knew how old he was either, but Cockroft had thought he had looked about two when he had appeared in the kitchen in the middle of a storm, his tail between his legs and his saturated fur accentuating his pitifully skinny ribs. That had been five years before, and thus he became seven.

From a distance there wasn't much to distinguish Timoleon Vieta from any of the other mongrels in Umbria. He was black with occasional spots of white and tan, and of average size, maybe a little smaller. But close to, he was somehow different from the others. He was very well looked after for a start, even indulged. He was no longer anywhere near as skinny as the Perugia strays, his nose shone with moisture and his coat, while being of various, apparently random lengths, was glossy and clean.

And there was something else that stood out about him – something that made him particularly unusual, and different even from other strays who had unwittingly stumbled into good homes. For although he was a mongrel, Timoleon Vieta's eyes were as pretty as a little girl's.

COCKROFT

Cockroft had spoken to nobody but Timoleon Vieta for a long time. Nobody had dropped by, and nobody had called. His last fully-fledged conversation had been on the phone to his accountant back in England, six days previously. It had started with a discussion of the small pension he had recently started to draw, and which made him feel so incredibly old, and ended with an argument over an aria, and the slamming down of a receiver. He had been drunk, and couldn't remember which of them it was who had done the slamming down this time, or even which aria it had been that one or other of them had deemed too strident, but it made little difference. In happier times they had been friends and sparring partners, and had cheerfully lost evenings attacking and defending the works of various musicians, conductors and composers over bottles of wine. But not any more. Now they just got on each other's nerves, and she had become no more than the person who managed his dwindling financial interests. The pension was enough to keep him alive and the roof free of holes, and a trickle of royalties from music he had written or arranged kept him in diesel, wine, cigars and the occasional weekend away, and just about stretched to the upkeep of a mongrel.

Timoleon Vieta was the fourth dog Cockroft had owned in the fifteen years he had been at the old stone farmhouse. He had lost the other three. The first, a red setter, had reacted badly to some pills and died in his arms of thrombosis at the age of seventeen months. The second, a Dalmatian, he had killed in a rage. His then boyfriend, a middle-aged Austrian music publisher whose name had slipped from memory but whose big grey moustache and fierce, hooded eyes lingered on, had just announced that he was going to sleep in the spare room that night, and that Cockroft could suck his own stupid penis for a change. This had been the culmination of hours of bickering, and Cockroft had hurled a heavy glass ashtray across the room. He had never meant to hit Jurgen, or Fritz, or whatever his name was, but merely to register his fury. It had, after all, been the Austrian's favourite ashtray, and its destruction would have been an incredible blow to him. It had carried a picture of a foaming stein, and he had loved it so much he had brought it with him all the way from Klagenfurt. The way he cherished it made it seem as though flicking the ash of his enormous cigars into any other receptacle would have nullified any pleasure gleaned from the smoke. It hit the ceiling and crashed down on to the Dalmatian's head, fracturing its skull. The Austrian drove away the next day, taking his unaccountably unscarred ashtray with him. Though they had started by talking so romantically of blood tests and joint accounts, it had run its course in less than six weeks.

The other dog, a Samoyed, had simply vanished. Cockroft remembered somebody telling him that the Italians secretly ate dogs, but he tried not to think about it. He preferred to think of her being gently picked up by a breeze and blown back to the Arctic Circle, like a little cloud.

Unable to face any more such heartache, Cockroft had decided never to own another dog. But the house seemed lonely without one, particularly during the long months he spent living alone, so when Timoleon Vieta had arrived, four years almost to the week after the disappearance of the Samoyed, it was as if the stork had brought him. He became the centre of Cockroft's world, and was lavished with food, comfort, attention and love. And in return Timoleon Vieta stayed with him, largely going about his business on his own, but occasionally returning to his master's side, wagging his tail and looking up at him, his head cocked to one side, with those irresistible eyes.

The house stood halfway up a hill, about two kilometres from the nearest proper road and a few minutes walk from the next house. Timoleon Vieta spent his days roaming around, and whenever he began to feel tired or hungry he returned to a big bowl of food, a comfortable armchair or patch of grass, warmth or shade depending on the weather, and the loving fuss of his first real owner. And for five years he had remained unshakably loyal. Men had come and gone. Young ones and old ones. Nice ones who had broken Cockroft's heart, and nasty ones who had broken his heart and stolen his belongings. Smooth pretty ones and big hairy ones. But the dog remained, through even the most trying of times. 'Timoleon Vieta,' Cockroft would say to him when they were alone again after another romantic apocalypse, 'you are a saint.'

Sharing every thing sweet and delicious with lovely master

THE BOSNIAN

They were sitting in front of the house, Cockroft in his deckchair and Timoleon Vieta by his side. It was a warm evening in early spring, and everything was quiet except for the rustling of a packet of nuts and raisins, and Timoleon Vieta's occasional wolfing of rejected Brazils.

Cockroft was trying to remember whether or not he had already told Timoleon Vieta about the time in the mid-sixties when he and Monty 'Misty' Moore had written *Wrens*, a stage musical for all ages about a good-hearted but misguided scientist who was secretly breeding killer wrens the size of emperor penguins in his underground laboratory. Thanks to Monty 'Misty' Moore's treachery it hadn't come close to being staged. Before he started to tell the story, regardless of whether or not the dog had heard it before, he was unexpectedly delighted by the sight of a scruffy, but handsome, young man walking up the track that ran in front of the house. 'That's funny,' he said, stroking his fussily trimmed silver beard. 'Who do you think this could be?' Timoleon Vieta's eyes were fixed on the raisin that had stalled halfway between the bag and his master's mouth.

The cars and jeeps of distant neighbours occasionally went past, but walkers never did. This one appeared to be somewhere around his mid-twenties. He was at least six feet tall, and was wearing old black jeans and a greying black T-shirt that was mottled with sweat. He was carrying a black bag, and his dark hair was looking, rather wonderfully, in pressing need of a cut. At times like these Cockroft kicked himself for knowing next to no Italian. 'Rough stuff,' he confided to Timoleon Vieta.

He smiled and waved at the young man, who didn't smile or wave back, but left the track and walked up the path toward the house. Cockroft had been expecting him to carry on up the track, and was surprised when he stopped just a few feet away from him.

'I have walked from the town,' he said quietly, looking not at Cockroft but at the house. 'You should have told me you lived such a long way from everywhere.' He dropped his bag on the ground, and there was a silence as he continued to scrutinise the house through narrowed eyes. 'But I am here now.' From deep inside the dog came the low rumble of a growl.

'Oh, be quiet Timoleon Vieta. Really,' admonished his master. 'What have I told you about behaving in front of visitors?' The dog backed away, but still quietly growled to himself. Cockroft rolled his eyes and shook his head in exaggerated exasperation, stood up and offered his hand. The young man took it. It felt clammy, and he wondered whether the old man had been playing with himself.

'So,' said Cockroft, trying his best to hide his confusion, 'you have my number.'

'Here.' He dug into his pocket, and brought out a card. On it was printed: *Carthusians Cockroft – conductor, composer, raconteur.* Underneath was his address and phone number. On his weekends away Cockroft gave them out like confetti – to handsome waiters, to gondoliers, to strangers he found himself talking to in art gallery snack bars and in museums, and to almost everyone he introduced himself to on his trips around the bars. The card was always accompanied by an open invitation to visit him at home. A few times over the years people had taken him up on his offer of hospitality in the hills, but they had usually called first to make sure he was going to be in. They didn't just arrive. 'You gave it in Firenze,' he said, his voice monotonous and barely audible. 'When you invited me.'

'Oh,' said Cockroft. 'Yes.' He tried to place the stranger's face, but he couldn't. 'Of course' he said, smiling as broadly as he could. 'It's so lovely to see you again. I was hoping you could make it.'

'I am thirsty. It was a long walk from the

town. Maybe one hour. More. Maybe five or six kilometres. I don't know.'

'Of course. Where are my manners? Do sit down.' He gestured towards his deckchair. As the young man moved towards it Timoleon Vieta exploded with rage, his hackles raised and his barks piercing the still evening air. 'Oh, Timoleon Vieta, please,' said Cockroft, almost firmly. Again Timoleon Vieta moved away and lay down, but he resumed his low growl. Cockroft went into the house.

After a couple of minutes the old man came back out, carrying a tray on which were four glasses, a jug of water, a bottle of sparkling wine and a plate full of chocolate biscuits. By the time Cockroft had assembled the spare deckchair, the young man had drunk all the water straight from the jug and poured himself a glass of wine, having fired the cork over the scruffy lawn and on to the track. Timoleon Vieta usually chased and returned fired corks, but this time his half-closed eyes didn't leave the newcomer's face.

'You *are* thirsty,' said Cockroft. The man did not respond.

Cockroft poured himself a glass of wine and sat down. From the corner of his eye he continued his inspection of the unexpected visitor. He was almost muscular, and looked weather-beaten and tired. Cockroft wanted to prescribe a rest cure: lots of relaxation, a bit of feeding up, and a lot of very close attention. He went to Florence every once in a while, and tried hard to remember having met the man there. His last couple of trips to the city had been blurs of sex, wine and tiramisu. He was sure he hadn't slept with him though. He would have remembered such a young, firm body. As he looked at the man in the deckchair beside him he was driven half wild with frustration. He wondered whether somebody such as this could ever even have heard of people like him. *What?* the young man would cry, slapping his thigh and laughing as Cockroft told him of their existence. *You mean there are men who kiss other men? And enjoy doing it? Oh Cockroft, you come up with the funniest ideas. I've never heard anything so preposterous in all my life, you old comedian.* Or maybe he would just stare at the distant hills, as he was doing now, and mumble without a smile, *Well, nothing surprises me any more.* Either way, Cockroft was sure he was out of luck.

The man grabbed a handful of biscuits from the plate and stuffed them into his mouth whole, not waiting until he had swallowed the first before eating the next. Cockroft took two – one for himself and one for Timoleon Vieta.

Cockroft handed the man a cigar, and started imagining they were long-term lovers enjoying a drink and a smoke as the sun went down over the distant hills, and about to enjoy a little, maybe post-coital, chit-chat. He didn't know what to say. He couldn't ask him his name, or where exactly it was they had met without appearing rude. 'So,' he said, after a lot consideration. 'Where are you from again?' Cockroft wasn't very good at telling where people were from by looking at them, but it was clear that the man was not Italian. He could tell from his accent.

'I told you already in Firenze,' he said. He paused for a long time. Then, in a broken whisper, he said, 'I am from Bosnia.'

'Oh, you poor boy. You poor, poor boy.' Most of Cockroft's life was played out before the backdrop of the World Service. It played on the kitchen radio almost every waking hour, and he knew all there was to know about the terrible things that were happening in what had once been Yugoslavia. At least until this conversation he had thought he had known everything. He certainly knew the names and places. *Slobodan Milosevic. Sarajevo. U.N. Peace Keeping Force. Mostar. Radavan Karadic. Mujahedin. Kosovo. Vance-Owen.* He seemed to know everything except, now he came to think about it, who had been fighting whom, who was on which side, what the sides were, which ethnicities were being cleansed, and what the various wars had all been about. He only occasionally read the papers, and tended to daydream through the main news events as they were broadcast on the radio, catching only the barest of outlines. He only ever paid close attention to the short pieces that rounded off the bulletins – like the report about the nine- year-old golf prodigy who had lost an arm in a fairground accident, or the woman who had fallen in love with her rapist and was struggling to have the charges against him dropped, or the man from somewhere outside Osaka who was lobbying *The Guinness Book of Records* to be entered as the loneliest man in the world. He had never really been able to untangle what had been going on just a short way to the east, and events had become so complex that without really thinking about it he had given up even trying to work them out.

He didn't know what to say, but felt as though he had to say something. He tried: 'Which side were you on?' He was sure the answer would mean nothing to him.

The Bosnian stared into the distance, seeming to be focusing on a point a long way beyond the horizon that Cockroft assumed was his ravaged homeland. Eventually he spoke, almost inaudibly. 'The side,' he said, 'with the guns.'

'Oh, you poor boy,' Cockroft repeated. He wanted to reach out and pat his hand. His strong hand, with its big, slightly dirty fingers. 'As I was saying to Timoleon Vieta the other day, I can never understand why people can't just get along

19

with each other. It seems so silly, all this fighting.'
He held out the bottle. 'More?'

Without taking his eyes from the view, the
Bosnian nodded almost imperceptibly, and Cockroft
poured two more glasses. It was almost like drinking champagne.

After a bowl of pasta, a few more cigars and glasses
of wine and a large glass of brandy, the Bosnian
was shown to the guest bedroom, where he fell
asleep on dusty sheets. Cockroft packed up the
deckchairs, read for a while, kissed Timoleon Vieta
goodnight and went to bed pleased that he would
have somebody to talk to in the morning.

TOOLS

Cockroft was woken by a scrabbling sound coming from outside his window. He put on his dressing gown, drew the curtain, craned his neck and could just make out the Bosnian fixing some guttering which had blown loose in a storm a few months before.

The Bosnian was tired of sleeping on beaches and in other people's tents, and the last of his money had been drained by the cheap hotels he had stayed in during the winter, when he couldn't find anybody to bunk up with and it had been too cold to stay out all night in a sleeping bag. He was tired of having to move all the time, worrying that if he stayed in one place for too long people would get suspicious of him. He wanted to spend some time in a place where there was no chance of seeing anyone he knew, where he wouldn't always be looking over his shoulder, where he could relax and do nothing at all, not even think. Where he could just be quietly, luxuriously bored. After waking early and taking a walk around the area he had decided to stay with the old man for at least a few days. The spare bed was comfortable, the food was free, and there was no immediate next door neighbour to ask him awkward questions. He was sure he had found somewhere he would be able to be bored with very little difficulty.

He wasted no time in finding an easy, high-profile job and very slowly getting on with it. He knew this would secure him at least a few days. Tying the gutter in place took a few minutes, and it made the house look tidier. He didn't mind the house too much. The only things he didn't like about his new home were the growling dog and the way of paying his rent that he had arranged with the old man when he had met him in Florence.

But he didn't have to think about the rent until Wednesday, so he put it to the back of his mind. Wednesday was the day they had arranged.

During dinner the night before the dog had glared hard at him through his half-closed eyes, only ever looking away to eat the scraps thrown by the old man.

Cockroft couldn't believe his luck at having stumbled across a young, handsome guest who undertook home repairs without having to be asked. He rewarded his labourer by making a huge breakfast. When it was ready, he called him inside for it. The Bosnian was still up the ladder, doing nothing but pretending he was still at work.

'I was just fixing the . . .' He pointed.

'Gutter.'

'Garder?'

'Gutter. Gu-tter.'

'Fixing the gutter. Gu-tter.'

'So I see. Thank you so much. I've been meaning to fix it myself, but . . .'

'You are old. You go up the ladder and you will

23

fall and you will be breaking your spine.' He made a cracking sound with his mouth.

'I'm not *that* old.' Cockroft was confident he could have passed for sixty-one. He still had a full head of hair, even if it was brilliant white, and although he was overweight he wasn't nearly as fat as a lot of his contemporaries. Even so, he was delighted that the Bosnian cared so much about his well-being.

They ate. Timoleon Vieta came in from outside and caught the scraps of bacon rind and crusts of fried bread thrown by his master.

'So do you like it here?' asked Cockroft.

The Bosnian didn't answer. He didn't want to be drawn into a conversation about how much he liked, or didn't like, the old man's house, so he changed the subject. 'You are having good tools,' he said. He had found a box of what looked like virtually unused tools in the cupboard under the sink. Some of them he didn't recognise, so they must have been specialist and expensive. 'Your house it is falling down and you are having tools. Look at this,' he said, walking over to the sink and picking a big splinter of rotten wood from the window sill. 'You are not using these tools.'

'Well, you know,' said Cockroft. 'It's so hard to find the time for DIY.' Cockroft, who never had a great deal to do, rarely thought about them. They had been left behind by a smooth-skinned and mildly aristocratic music student whom he had unexpectedly managed to seduce on a trip back to England. In their love prattle they had dreamed up the idea of the student coming over to Italy in his summer holiday, where he would work on the house by day and make love to Cockroft by night. Cockroft, having been blind drunk during this conversation, had promptly forgotten the arrangement, so when the boy had arrived on his doorstep on the day they had agreed, it had come as a surprise. He had been entertaining a policeman, who saw himself and the Englishman as a steady couple despite having a wife and only seeing his lover two afternoons a week, when he was supposed to be stopping cars down on the main road. The policeman, who had just changed back into his uniform, pulled his gun from its holster, pointed it at the music student's head and ordered him back the way he had come. The student knew no Italian, but realised he had lost an unexpected battle for the old man's affections. The taxi that had dropped him off had gone, so he had to run. He dropped the box of tools he had brought with him, and which must have been hell to get over on the plane.

Though he had been excited to have had men fighting over him with guns, Cockroft remembered just how handsome the student had been, how in certain lights his eyes had been almost violet, and how enthusiastically and affectionately he had thrown himself into his first fling with an older man. He wished he had stopped the policeman, and called the terrified boy back. He would have had such a wonderful time if he had stayed. He later heard that he had found refuge in a Tuscan bar where he had been picked up by, of course, Monty 'Misty' Moore. By the time the story reached Cockroft, it had Monty 'Misty' Moore buying his new friend several sets of cricket whites, and spending the summer treating him to cocktails, watching him splash around in his pool, and poisoning every corner of his mind against Cockroft. And things were never the same between the old man and the policeman after that episode. Before long the visits dried up.

All day the Bosnian kept himself looking busy by fiddling around with the tools, tightening screws and oiling hinges. They were easy, obvious jobs that required little thought or effort, but enabled him to appear so deep in concentration that conversation would not be possible. He wanted to avoid listening to the old man as much as he could. Almost everything the Bosnian had heard him say had been white noise.

In the late afternoon Cockroft celebrated the small improvements to his home by bringing out a pair of very large gin and tonics. They sat in the deckchairs.

Cockroft wanted to know everything about his new housemate. 'So,' he began, his English slow and precise. 'How long have you been in Italy?'

It was a long time before the Bosnian answered.

He was breathing very, very slowly. Cockroft was wondering whether or not to ask the question again when the young man answered. He said, 'Two year.'

'How did you get here?'

'Boat.' He had been through the ordeal of this conversation many times before.

'Oh, how wonderful. Isn't the Adriatic lovely? Where did you land?'

'On somewhere. By the sea, with the sand.'

'Oh, on a beach.'

'A beach,' he mumbled to himself, as though it were the first time he had used the word. 'A beach.'

'And were you caught by the police?'

'No.'

Cockroft was captivated by his new friend's answers. He was convinced that the Bosnian carried deep emotional scars, and that with time and friendship he would be able to open up. He pictured the young man breaking down at the recollection of being held captive behind enemy lines for months on end, or seeing his best friend killed in battle. He saw the Bosnian in floods of tears, falling into his comforting arms and yielding to his caresses.

'I run away. Before the police was arriving.'

They drank their drinks, smoked cigarettes and looked at the view. Cockroft knew he was going to live in that house for the rest of his life, and that he would probably die sitting in a deckchair and looking out at the distant hills. A hot air balloon came into view. It was red, black and beautiful. It must have been about half a mile away. He imagined he was in the basket with the Bosnian. Just the two of them, huddled together and floating almost motionless in the evening sky. The Bosnian was holding him tight in his strong arms, and placing the occasional gentle kiss on his face. *I love you Cockroft*, he was saying. *I love you so much.*

Suddenly a panel tore off the balloon. It began to deflate. It started to spin and buck, and headed towards the ground. The basket tipped, and two tiny figures fell out, first one and then the other. They seemed to fall slowly and gently, as though they would land softly and unharmed on the ground below. The empty basket was spinning wildly as the balloon descended.

'Oh dear,' said Cockroft.

FIGHT

Because Wednesday had been agreed in Florence as rent day, the Bosnian had made sure he arrived at Cockroft's house on a Thursday. That gave him almost a week to decide whether or not he was going to pay. On the Monday the old man noticed that his guest had been wearing the same clothes all that time, and that they needed washing.

'Come along,' he said. 'We're getting you some new clothes from the market.' Cockroft filled his wallet, and went out to make sure the pick-up was going to start. He had bought the small white four-wheel-drive secondhand when he had moved to Italy, convinced that he would need a rugged machine for his new rural lifestyle. It had become as run-down as the house, but it was inexplicably reliable. He also had a little Fiat in his garage, but he had never really liked it, and anyway it hadn't worked for months. He half-wondered whether the Bosnian could get it going again. His new friend seemed to Cockroft to be the kind of person who could fix a car. As usual the pick-up started first time, and he left it ticking over. 'I'll just call Timoleon Vieta,' he said.

The Bosnian didn't say anything, he just looked away.

'Yes, he loves his trips into town.' He called the dog's name a few times. Eventually he appeared. 'We go everywhere together, don't we Timoleon Vieta?' The dog started scratching at the passenger door. 'Ah. I'd forgotten about that. There's a slight problem. You see, Timoleon Vieta likes to sit in the passenger seat.'

'But there is no problem. He will go into the back.'

'Oh no. He won't be happy in the back.'

'He is dog, right? He is animal?'

'He's fine in the back of the car, but he doesn't

like it in the back of the pick-up, you know. He finds it uncomfortable.' The Bosnian was looking into the distance, seeming to see and hear nothing. 'But I'll see what I can do.' Cockroft lowered the pick-up's back flap and said, in a well-practised falsetto, 'Jump. Jump. Jump up, Timoleon Vieta.' The dog lay down. 'Jump up.' Timoleon Vieta curled up and closed his eyes. 'No. It's no use. He'll have to come in the front with me.'

'Why not do like this?' The Bosnian went up to Timoleon Vieta, and bent down to pick him up and bundle him into the back. He swept him up, and the moment he did the dog turned from a listless mound into a flailing, yapping whirl of claws and teeth. The Bosnian dropped him. Timoleon Vieta retreated to a safe distance, where he growled and raised his hackles at his master's new friend, who was wiping the dog's saliva on to his jeans, and checking his hand for punctures.

'Let's go,' said the Bosnian. He hadn't wanted to make the trip but had started to be bothered by his own stench, so he had decided to go along with the old man's plan. 'We leave the dog here. He is surviving here no problem.'

'Oh, please let him sit in the front,' implored Cockroft. 'You can go in the back. It'll be fun. It'll be just like your army days all over again.' The Bosnian, who had decided that he would really rather not have to talk to the old man anyway, climbed up without another word. Cockroft worried that he had been tactless. He pictured a rainy night, an explosion, and the Bosnian being thrown from the back of a jeep into a quagmire while his comrades lost limbs around him. The old man and his dog got in the front. Cockroft patted Timoleon Vieta's head. Timoleon Vieta looked up at him with his lovely eyes, and wagged his tail. They went into town, Cockroft taking the bends very slowly.

After parking, and leaving Timoleon Vieta in the cab of the pick-up, they went to the hardware store, to the bank and to the market to buy the clothes. At the market the Bosnian performed all the negotiations in what seemed to Cockroft to be fluent Italian. The old man ended up buying him a couple of pairs of jeans, a pair of what looked like army boots, a bundle of underwear, some plain T-shirts and some big work shirts. He steered him towards colours that matched his eyes. The Bosnian asked for, and was given, a hat and a pair of dark glasses, both of which he put on immediately. 'I must be being careful,' he said, without smiling. 'I am not supposed to be being around here.'

They took the bags back to the pick-up, via a cheap barber where Cockroft watched the Bosnian have his head shaved, number one all over. Exhausted, Cockroft suggested they go for a cup of coffee.

The Bosnian needed caffeine. 'I suppose you will be wanting that dog to come with us,' he mumbled.

Cockroft had wanted Timoleon Vieta's company, but he stalled. 'No. He can stay and guard our bags. He'll be fine, so long as we're quick.' Guiltily, he warmed to the idea of having a coffee with just the Bosnian, and he felt a slight buzz as he realised he was being seen out and about with an authentic fugitive. Over his years in Italy he had known plenty of people who shouldn't really have been in the country. They had been Russians, Micronesians, Peruvians and Americans – the chiselled boyfriends of rich ex-patriates and Italians. Still, he was sure none of them had been a refugee from a war zone. He had never known the illegal people he had met to get caught, so he wasn't too worried about his new friend being snatched away from him by the police. He was sure he would get away with it somehow, just like all the others. Even so, it was quite exciting for the old man.

The cafe was Cockroft's favourite in town, but he wasn't sure why. The staff never showed any signs of recognition when he arrived. They just served him with whatever it was he had asked for, and took his money. He and the Bosnian took a table outside, and ordered a pair of cappuccinos. The Bosnian smoked cheap cigarettes, and the old man smoked cheap cigars. Neither of them spoke.

An argument broke out on the other side of the street. Two men, both with pot bellies and moustaches, were shouting insults at each other, and waving their arms. People walked by as though nothing unusual were happening. 'They are a very expressive race, the Italians,' explained Cockroft. 'You know, they never fight. They use all their energy waving their arms around and shouting at each other, and so they don't feel the need to fight one another.'

One of the men, who was wearing a blue shirt, started poking the chest of the other one, who was wearing a white shirt. 'There might be a bit of poking,' conceded the old man, 'but that's all. It never gets serious.'

The white-shirted man answered these pokes with a punch so hard that it knocked the blue-shirted one to the ground. Blue-shirt got up, clearly dazed, and rubbed his head. The shouting had been succeeded by silence, and they no longer waved their arms so expressively. White-shirt followed up on his success, and landed another punch on blue-shirt's face. Blood ran from blue-shirt's nose, and this seemed to snap him back into life. In a moment, white-shirt had been knocked to the ground, and was being kicked in the belly over and over again. He rolled over, but blue-shirt kept on kicking, his shoes pounding into the other man's back as he struggled to stand up.

'Oh really,' said Cockroft. 'This is no way to behave.'

'I have not seen this for the long while,' muttered the Bosnian. He seemed to be smiling, but the old man wasn't entirely sure. 'It is so beautiful.'

'How can you say that? It's awful. It's mindless violence.'

'But it is not without reasons.' Looking at the fight and not at Cockroft, his voice barely above a whisper, he seemed to be talking to himself. 'We will never know just what it is in these lifes that is driving these people to this. It is more than the simple fighting in the street − it is two lifes, two of the histories on collision. The reasons for this fight is going back for so many, many generations.' He looked, for a moment, at the old man. 'Think about it.'

It was the first time Cockroft had seen the Bosnian seem interested in something. 'Well, whatever their reasons may be, there is never any need for violence.' Cockroft had never been in a fight. Not a real one, with fists. Blue-shirt had white-shirt's hair in his hand, and was knocking his head against a wall.

'But a fight between two men is the most purest form of all conflict. It is simple, and it is beautiful. It is perfect.'

'But they have no dignity, these men.'

'No what?'

'No dignity.'

'What means this word? This *dignity*?' asked the Bosnian.

'Well,' said Cockroft. His mind went blank. 'It's difficult to explain.'

'But you are using this word,' mumbled the Bosnian. 'I think you are knowing what it means if you are using it.'

'Well,' Cockroft thought for a moment. 'It means behaving yourself no matter what.'

'Are you sure?' They watched as white-shirt

wrestled free, and stood a little way away from blue-shirt, catching his breath, his moustache caked with blood.

'Yes. And it means having self-control, and not making an exhibition of yourself.'

'So do you have this dignity?'

'I like to think so. Yes, I do.' Even though the more he thought about it the more he realised he wasn't quite sure what it meant, Cockroft knew that there had been times when he had lost his dignity completely. He wondered whether it was possible for somebody to lose it in private, or whether somebody else had to be watching for it to count. He wondered whether he had lost his dignity on the summer night he had spent doing the conga alone, wearing nothing but a paper hat from a Christmas cracker, or the time when he had heard on the radio that household dust was in large part flakes of human skin, and had spent hours carefully collecting dust and putting it in a jar so that he might have something by which to remember the object of a recently failed love whom, in his happiness, he had neglected to photograph. He knew for certain that he had lost it in 1976 when, during a particularly difficult time in his life, the police had caught him spraying *I SUCK COCKS* on a footbridge over a dual carriageway. When the incident wasn't reported in the newspapers he didn't know whether to feel disappointed or relieved.

'And am I having this dignity also?'

'Yes. I think you are.' Cockroft had no idea. White-shirt lunged at blue-shirt.

The Bosnian, having encountered the word many times before, smiled to himself for a moment, with just one side of his mouth. 'But you are saying that these men they are not having this dignity. Well maybe it is better if you are not having it. Fighting is better than not fighting when there is something to fight about. Maybe it is weak not to fight people. This fight it is so beautiful. Like a fucking, I don't know, like a fucking picture or something.'

'It is *not* beautiful.'

'It is beautiful.'

The conversation, in which they had both lost

interest, ended. Their attention returned to the fight.

After a couple more minutes of grappling, headbutting, kicking and pummelling, blue-shirt walked away, leaving white-shirt lying still on the pavement. Cockroft and the Bosnian made their way back to the pick-up.

The Bosnian supposed that the fight had been about a girl – he was sure he had seen the fire of love in the men's eyes. He imagined what she must have been like to have inspired such violence. He pictured her long dark hair cascading over her bare shoulders, her enormous brown eyes and her perfect body. She was far too good for either of them. What she was doing hanging around with those pot-bellied men he would never understand. She was beautiful, and he tried not to think about it.

They drove back to the house, Timoleon Vieta on the passenger seat and the Bosnian lying down in the fresh air.

Cockroft rarely felt it was worth making a special effort in the kitchen when there was only him and Timoleon Vieta in the house. Usually he just grazed on bread, fruit and nuts through the day and made a simple pasta dish in the evening, but whenever he had a visitor he rediscovered his culinary enthusiasm. He stopped off at the supermarket for some bits and pieces on the way back from town.

Despite the enormous and meticulously prepared meal, the atmosphere at the table was not what Cockroft had hoped for. The Bosnian, in his new clothes, was quiet, seeming intent on his meal. He answered Cockroft's questions with gestures or the minimum of words. The old man worried that he had spoiled everything by making him sit in the back of the pick-up. The World Service filled the silences.

'You speak very good English,' said Cockroft, hoping to regain lost ground.

'It is so-so,' said the Bosnian, who knew that his English was good.

After the meal the old man poured a pair of very large whiskeys, and showed the Bosnian the music room for the first time. It was Cockroft's favourite room. 'I keep it very tidy,' he said. 'I don't even let Timoleon Vieta sit on the chairs.'

'Then you will not let me sit on the fucking chairs,' the Bosnian said, without raising his voice from its usual, almost whispered, monotone. 'I am below your dog.'

Cockroft was embarrassed. He had not been a good host. He had treated the Bosnian thoughtlessly. He supposed that his world had become so small that he had simply forgotten how to treat guests, that he should have put the Bosnian's needs above everything else. He knew he should have broken his and Timoleon Vieta's routine without hesitation, and he was ashamed. 'I'm so sorry,' he said. 'Listen. You can sit in the front of the pick-up next time we go somewhere, and I'll put Timoleon Vieta in the back. I'll make him jump up whether he likes it or not. I'll throw a biscuit up there or something.' Cockroft didn't know what else to say, so he said, 'He loves biscuits.'

The Bosnian didn't respond to this gesture. He looked around the room. There was an upright piano with its lid down, and a black leather sofa and matching armchair, and the walls were covered with framed photographs. Cockroft rarely played the piano, a dusty Spelman Timmins that he had shipped over from home shortly after buying the place in the hope that he would hit another creative patch. He never did. His musical about Crufts had never really come together. He had abandoned it halfway through the fifth song, which had been about a basset. His classical piece, *Rape Of The Seas*, which he had started to write during a phase of refusing to eat fish, had foundered after he was offered salmon at a dinner party. He had forgotten to tell the host about his diet, and the fish had smelled so good that he had been unable to resist it. He hadn't had the piano tuned since the local blind man had died seven years before, so whatever he played on it sounded somehow diabolical. The Bosnian walked around and looked at the photographs. In the middle of them all was a big photograph of someone who was recognisably Cockroft in conversation with Paul McCartney. Cockroft, trying hard not to swell too obviously with pride, pointed at it without saying anything.

'McCartney,' said the Bosnian.

'Yes.'

'He is coming from The Wings.'

'Yes.'

'I fucking hate The Wings.' The Bosnian sang, quietly, sarcastically and without tune, *We are sailing . . .*'

'Yes, I think that was them.'

'Fucking shit.' He curled his lip slightly. 'I suppose he is your good friend.'

'Yes, he is. He's a lovely man.' Cockroft had met him twice – in passing in Jane Asher's hallway in 1964, when he had been on his way to meet her brother Peter to talk about the possibility of arranging some music for a flip side, and again when that picture had been taken, in 1973. On their second meeting they had had a thirty second conversation in which Cockroft had reminded McCartney of their earlier encounter, and commented on how Jane Asher's house had smelled of lovely cakes. McCartney had smiled politely, then moved away.

'A really super fellow, Paul. A charming man. A good friend.'

Putting their difference of opinion about Wings down to a culture clash, the old man talked the Bosnian through some of the other photographs. There was a younger Cockroft with a very young David Bowie, with a tired-looking Jimi Hendrix, and standing on the left of a group that included Sammy Davis Junior. A few of the photographs were formal shots, in which Cockroft had a baton in his hand and was surrounded by men in matching blazers clutching electric basses, drumsticks or violins. 'I had my own little orchestra,' he said, pointing at one of the pictures. 'I was a bandleader. I used to be on television all the time. I even made records.' The Bosnian didn't say anything.

They went back to the kitchen table. Cockroft poured even more whiskey into their glasses. 'I'm very famous in my own country, you know,' he said. 'Very famous indeed.'

'Bullshit,' thought the Bosnian, who had never heard of him.

*　　*　　*

After the Bosnian had gone to bed Cockroft sat with his elbows on the kitchen table, drinking wine and looking at his reflection in the rough old glass of the window. He felt Timoleon Vieta nuzzling him. He slid his chair back, reached down and stroked the dog's head. 'Come here,' he said, drawing the dog into an embrace. After a while the old man kissed him on his muzzle, and withdrew. Then he gently held the dog's head in his hands, and played with his ears. Timoleon Vieta looked up at him with his pretty eyes, tilted his head to one side and wagged his tail.

'Come here,' Cockroft said again, reaching down to hug his pet.

SILVER SHORTS

There were framed photographs of men here and there around the house. Most of them looked fairly anonymous. There was a fey, scholarly looking young man in spectacles and white trousers, and a muscular, middle-aged black man in extraordinarily tight swimming trunks. There was the seventeen-year-old from Holland who had kept telling the old man to grow up, and the man from the Falkland Islands who had packed his bags and left shortly after Cockroft had found him in the kitchen in the early hours of the morning, masturbating into the electric fan. Cockroft had supposed that the spots that had begun to appear on the table, the wall and the ceiling had been some sort of Italian fungus. Most of the men were only represented once, but the Bosnian felt one pair of eyes following him wherever he went. He was in the bathroom, in the kitchen at least twice, on top of the piano, in various corridors and in the living room. He looked young, not much more than a boy. In some photos he was alone, in others he was standing next to the old man, and in others he was draped all over the dog. In the one in the bathroom he was naked except for a very small towel, in another he was wearing a sailor suit, and in at least three of them he was wearing a pair of skin-tight silver shorts. The Bosnian thought his legs looked like a girl's.

The boy in the silver shorts had liked the company of older men. 'You know,' he had said to Cockroft, breaking off from their first kiss, 'I won't even look at a boy unless he's forty years older than I am. I never have done and I never will. I dread the day when I'm sixty years old and I have to hunt around for a pretty boy who's a hundred. And I like you. I like you English boys a lot. I like your voices.'

When they first met, the boy had been the house guest of an eighty-six-year-old Swiss financier. Cockroft had been invited to a party at their house, and had assumed that this glorious, long-legged vision, distributing vol-au-vents and captivating everybody with his combination of southern American charm and the fluent Italian he had learned from his mother, had been a gold digger. He later found out that the boy didn't care too much about money. He had inherited just about enough to keep himself in tight clothes without having to go to work, and that was all he needed. Short shorts, two passports and an elderly boyfriend to love until he got bored of loving him and took his long legs, fine golden hair and smooth skin to another old man's bed. He proved this by leaving the rich Swiss man before the old boy had had a chance to die and leave him any of his money, and moving in with a disgraced, virtually friendless and relatively impoverished conductor, whose eyes were still quite bright and who still had a full head of silver hair.

'You know, I like this place. It's a real home,' he

had said to Cockroft as he stood in the kitchen with his bags at his feet. 'It's not like that other place. We had everything there – a swimming pool, a tennis court, a sauna and everything, but it wasn't half as nice as this. It had no . . . you know. This is a real home. And that old boy, he was no fun at all. He was pretty enough, but all he'd do is lie around all day in that big old bed of ours. I like my boys to be as old as the hills, but they've got to have just a little bit of life left in them. And he didn't even let animals in the house. Can you believe that? He had a thing about it. I asked him if I could have just a tiny little kitty cat and he went crazy. Me, I like doggies best of all, and this doggy here is my favouritest little doggy in the whole wide window.' He pounced on Timoleon Vieta, who had been curled up on his chair and eyeing the stranger suspiciously, and made a fuss of him. He gave the dog a chunk of chocolate. Timoleon Vieta wagged his tail.

For four months Cockroft's life had been a whirl of happiness. The boy in the silver shorts would not stop talking, and as soon as Cockroft had developed a strategy for getting a word in edgeways they developed such a rapport that the days flew by. They made each other laugh, they shopped, they drove around, they played games, they sang songs, they pampered the dog, they drank wine and they had wonderful sex several times a day. It had almost been like the old days again, like the sixties, when everyone had known who he was. Back then people would cross crowded rooms to talk to him and be seen with him. He could go to a party alone, and know that within moments of arriving he would be holding court, and some of the most respected people in the country would be listening to him, laughing at his anecdotes and inviting him to their homes for dinner. Boys who wanted to be actors would invite themselves back to his flat in Fitzrovia, and he had always felt a sense of avuncular pride whenever any of them had found themselves parts in films or on television. He appeared regularly in newspapers' society pages, never missing an opportunity to be photographed next to beautiful girls called Alaska, Jezebella or Benin. He had not felt like that a single time since the night in 1974 when he had disgraced himself so publicly and so comprehensively. Since then he had felt awful almost all the time. But when he was with the boy in the silver shorts it was the sixties again. The part of him that he had assumed had died suddenly came alive again, and for the first time in years he was certain beyond doubt that he was in love.

Things were different with the Bosnian. In the few days he had been at the house he had hardly spoken. He didn't like the dog, and the dog didn't like him. He had no history of dressing up in gingham to seduce his uncles. He didn't bring out the best in Cockroft. And he liked girls. He had made that clear. 'I like the girls,' he had said, in his foreign voice. But the old man was happy enough to have him around the house. He could have spent hours watching him out of the corner of his eye as he lazily fixed doors or half-heartedly hacked at the undergrowth with their new scythe. Most importantly of all, he didn't even feel too sad when he thought about the boy in the silver shorts. A few weeks before he had spent a whole day crying over him, but at least now he had someone to look at, even if he would never get to touch him.

He tried to remember what life had been like in the days immediately before the Bosnian had walked up the track. It was a blur. Two or three months earlier he had been abandoned by an average-looking Frenchman after an indifferent affair that had lasted only a few weeks, and the time in between had seemed like a single interminable day, interrupted by sleep from which he would often jolt awake, startled by his own mediocrity. But the few days the Bosnian had been around had been a little bit different from each other. As much as he loved Timoleon Vieta, and hated to see him looking so down, Cockroft hoped his new friend would stay for a while.

UGLY WOMEN

When he was younger the Bosnian had dreamed of travelling the world and making love to the whores of many nations. Gradually though, he had realised that however far he travelled the girls he met would be pretty much the same. He had seen photographs and videos of prostitutes from around the world, and they all looked fairly similar – wearing a lot of make up, and dressed very well in high heels and short, tight skirts. Whether he was to go to Bangkok where you picked them up in bars, or Amsterdam where you more or less fucked them in shops, or New York where you called them on the phone and made appointments with them as though they were opticians, he knew the girls would be more or less the same kind of thing. So he didn't mind too much creeping between various innocuous addresses close to home and having sex with the girls who had left their towns and villages, and often even their countries, telling their families that they were going to find work as hotel receptionists or personal assistants, or in travel agencies and hospitals.

He had a friend who would never go with pretty whores because he knew he would fall in love with them. In the days when he would hire a beautiful girl it would break his heart to think that she didn't love him in return, and that she was only letting him touch her because he had enough money to be able to own her for an hour or two. Sometimes he spent the whole time just stroking the girl's hair, looking at her face from different angles, and telling her how beautiful she was while telling himself how much he loved her and how he wished things had been different between them. He wouldn't even get around to doing what he had paid to do – thinking that it was too soon and that they should take the time to get to know one another first. Afterwards, unable to stop thinking about her, he would write her a letter, to which he would not receive a reply. After too much heartache like this he had decided to go exclusively for the cheapest whores available. He always chose the one with the missing front tooth, the one with the big bags under her eyes, or the one who had been beaten so many times that her nose no longer knew which way to point. As well as saving him money, he would know from the start that he wasn't going to fall in love.

Although the Bosnian always went with the best-looking prostitutes he could afford, many of whom were almost unbelievably beautiful, with big sad eyes and perfect, airbrushed skin, he had encountered some ugly women too. On drunken nights out, when he had been about seventeen, he and his friends had sometimes competed with each other to see which of them could kiss, for at least two minutes, the ugliest woman. To make it difficult they weren't allowed to pay, so they had to go to bars and discos and other places where these women could be found. A couple of times he had won the contest. One night one of his friends had won in fine style, spending a whole evening with a woman that they all agreed was a contender for the all-time worst. A real stinker. Her face was all over the place, and she was fat. They watched them as they talked, and shortly after midnight their friend took her back to his room, where he made her pregnant. When the news broke they all got together and pooled as much money as he would need to pay for the abortion. They knew he didn't have as much money as they all did. When they offered it to him he went quiet.

'We've been talking,' he said. 'Me and that girl.' He looked at his shoes. 'We're getting married. We're getting married and having the baby.'

They couldn't understand. They just stared at him as he tried to explain. 'I like her,' he said. 'I know it sounds stupid, but I really like her. We've got lots in common. And she's really funny and things.'

They gave him the money anyway, for baby things, and some of them turned up to the wedding when it happened six weeks later. It was strange to see him standing there in his suit with this ugly girl next to him, wearing her white dress and with a child growing somewhere underneath her rolls of fat. Afterwards they drank beer and agreed that the whole business had been more like a funeral.

They sometimes saw him around from then on, as they sat outside bars or lay drinking in the park. 'Here he comes,' they would say. 'Here he comes with his ugly wife.' Their friend would carry his baby over and talk for a while, usually about things the child had done. Noises it had made. If his wife drifted out of earshot they invited him out drinking, but he always had an excuse. He would be looking after the baby, or making things for the small flat he shared with his new family. Muttering something about how the baby understood every word they said, or some such drivel, he would go away. 'There he goes,' they would say. 'There he goes with his ugly wife.'

It was with kissing ugly women in mind that the Bosnian went to pay his rent. He imagined it wouldn't be much different.

*   *   *

'We go inside now,' he said to Cockroft, who was sitting outside and patting Timoleon Vieta on the head while half re-reading *A Spy By Any Other Name* by Wadham Kenning. 'Now.' Cockroft followed him as he went in to the house. 'It is Wednesday. It is seven o'clock. Give me your cock.'

Cockroft knew instinctively that he must not show how amazed he was. It was a line he had used time and time again. *Come and visit me – all you'll have to do is suck my dick at seven o'clock on a Wednesday evening and you can stay as long as you like.* He had thought that everyone had known it was a joke, despite the well-practised poker face he always adopted while making the offer. But not the Bosnian. In Bosnia, it seemed, a deal was a deal and the Bosnian was ready to pay his rent. Not wanting Timoleon Vieta to see what was about to happen, he locked the front door, leaving him stuck outside.

Cockroft had lost track of how many hours of his life he had spent contemplating suicide. Once he had tried to do the maths, but the figure he had arrived at meant that he would have had to have spent over a hundred and six years, without sleeping, doing nothing but thinking about killing himself. Assuming he had misplaced a decimal point or something, he had given up, contenting himself with the knowledge that it was certainly a very long time.

He had always been mesmerised by news reports of suicides. He could never quite work out why people tended to kill themselves in such mundane ways – cutting their wrists in their bathrooms, gorging themselves with pills and Cinzano in their bedrooms, quietly gassing themselves in their kitchens or in car parks near beauty spots, dangling from banisters, shooting themselves with nobody there to watch the insides of their heads spray around the room or, like his daughter, discreetly toppling over cliffs on dark nights in November.

Cockroft's own suicide plans had always been much grander than the stories he read in the brief paragraphs of local newspapers. He saw himself hiding out in the Albert Hall, waiting for everybody to go home, somehow attaching a rope to the highest point of the ceiling and jumping from the top tier. His body would be discovered in the morning, hanging thirty or forty feet above the ground. Everybody would stand there and wonder how to get him down. News bulletins throughout the day would provide updates to an interested public as his body was somehow brought back down to earth. Rehearsals for the Proms would be disrupted. Sometimes he imagined himself running into one of Monty 'Misty' Moore's famous garden parties with a blunderbuss, crying, 'Look what you've done to me,' before pointing the gun at himself and spraying spots of his blood all over the men in their white flannel trousers. In another daydream he had thought about hanging himself from the high ceiling of an ex's loft bedroom with a noose made of cheese wire. The handsome, but fickle and stupid boy would bring a lover home to find the old man lying in two parts on his bed, his neck severed perfectly, sliced like the Caerphilly they had enjoyed so much on their two-week anniversary visit to Wales.

The closest Cockroft had ever come to really killing himself had been the time he had lain down on a beautiful stretch of railway line near Dawlish, and waited for a night train. He enjoyed the smell of the sea air and the feeling of the cold track against his neck. He looked at the stars. He had had a lot to drink, so they were fluttering around. It was a long time before he felt the steel vibrate. He had been about to fall asleep, but he immediately came to and climbed frantically to his feet, jumped well clear and stood petrified as the track began to sing. Much sooner than he had expected the train went past. His heart thumped wildly as he pictured his head flopping down on one side of the track and his feet on the other. He walked back to his bed and breakfast, worried about getting into trouble with the landlady. He had told her he would be back by half past ten, and she had seemed severe. The more he thought about it, the surer he became that he had been truly suicidal as he had lain there that night. He supposed he just hadn't quite been suicidal enough.

After that mundane near-attempt he always told himself that before ending his life he would try doing something extreme, just in case it were to inspire him to keep on living, to make him see the point. He had written a long list of things to seriously think about doing before killing himself. It had included covering the whole of his face and body with tattoos, having a small hole drilled in his cranium, joining a dating agency and meeting marriage-minded women, and going over Niagara Falls in a barrel. Another item on his list was selling his flat in London and buying an old house in the Italian countryside.

He often wondered why he had bothered, why he hadn't just stood outside *The Mousetrap* years ago, telling the arriving audience who the murderer was before walking across town and sneaking into the Albert Hall to set up his noose. But this was one of the rare moments when he was glad that he had never quite got around to ending it all. If he had done, he wouldn't be lying on the kitchen table, about to have his balls sucked dry by a big, handsome Bosnian.

Cockroft unbuttoned and unzipped his trousers, and got it out. The Bosnian looked at it as it stood half-proud, staring up at him with its single Mongoloid eye. He moved his face towards it, then pulled back. 'Shower,' he said. 'Take a shower before I do this.' He wasn't going to suck something that smelled of stale sweat and urine.

Obediently, Cockroft went to the bathroom. He emerged a while later in his bath robe. 'Come to the penetraleum,' he said. The Bosnian hadn't seen Cockroft's room before. He hadn't wanted to. They walked upstairs. There was a very big, unmade bed, and scattered around were more pictures of the old man's favourite – one of him in his silver shorts, and another of him entirely naked, lying on his front by a swimming pool with a cocktail in his hand. The old man lay on his back, his legs apart, the clean, unexpectedly excited little pink thing sticking up like an antenna from its bed of black and grey hairs. The Bosnian pressed his lips against its tip, then enveloped the whole thing with his mouth. The old man gasped. 'Less teeth. Less teeth,' he said.

'OK,' spluttered the Bosnian, the penis still in his mouth. He was trying to find the right angle of approach, and withdrew to reassess the situation.

'Don't stop – please. You're doing well.'

'Do not worry. I am making a new position. I will suck.' He put his mouth back down over the penis. It was easy now. He ran his tongue along it, and more or less kept his head still as the old man thrust up and down. Cockroft moaned and gasped, and roughly ran his fingers over the stubble on his new friend's head while at the same time pressing down to make sure those rough young lips didn't stray too far from his crotch.

After what seemed to the Bosnian to be an eternity the penis began to pulse, and he felt the warm, horrible liquid hit the back of his mouth. It quivered, and began to shrink. He started to withdraw his head, but Cockroft pushed him back down. 'There's more,' the old man gasped. A final squirt hit the roof of the Bosnian's mouth.

He pulled away, and swallowed. He walked down to the kitchen, where he drank a pint of water. He could still taste it, so he drank another pint. He could still taste it, so he went to find some toothpaste.

Cockroft lay on his bed in a state of disbelief. 'Oh,' he said. 'Ah.'

FROSTBITE

Cockroft had begun thinking about his annual trip to Gubbio long before the Bosnian had arrived, but the prospect of having a companion for the day had made him look forward to it all the more. When the day of the outing came, the Bosnian sat in Timoleon Vieta's traditional place on the passenger seat. The dog whined as his master tied him up in the back, and he was still whining as they drove away. Cockroft was worried. He was sure the dog knew what had been going on between his master and the young man, and did not approve.

In 1929, on the outskirts of a small town in the Alps, a mother had hated her new baby boy so much that she had taken him into the woods and left him lying in the snow. When her husband came home from work he was impatient to see his first child again, and he asked her where he was. She didn't answer. She just stared at the floor and hummed, humming louder and louder the more desperate her husband's inquiries became. Frantic, he beat her, his fists smashing into the face he thought the most beautiful in the world. Choking, and with blood running from her mouth, she told him what she had done. He called to his neighbours to help him look for the child. The word spread and men and boys came running out of their homes and their shops, leaving the women to look after the small children and to keep the fires burning. It was almost dark when they found him. He was colourless, and lying perfectly still. It was as though a new-born-baby-shaped icicle had fallen from a tree. They wrapped him in a coat and ran to the doctor, who had been told to prepare for the patient. Dismissing the men from his surgery, he set to work. Having sent the youngest boys home, the men crowded around the door, listening. When they heard the baby's feeble cry they leapt for joy. The father burst into the room and clutched his child to his chest.

The boy's recovery was not complete. Frostbite claimed the tip of his nose, half his toes and all the digits on his hands except for his left index finger. Everyone in the village made sure that his mother never went near him again. She pleaded and pleaded with her husband as he came to collect his belongings and move out of their house. She told him that she couldn't understand why she had done what she had done, that she felt so much better now, and that they should just forget about it and pretend it had never happened. He wouldn't acknowledge a word she said, and the wall of paternal relatives that guarded the child could not be breached. Sometimes she would catch sight of him and cry *My baby, my baby*, but he would be whisked out of harm's way before she could get close to him. Before long the father moved away, taking his son with him. Nobody would tell her where they had gone, only that they had gone a long way away and that she would not be seeing them again.

Her love for the boy drove her out of her mind. Able to think of nothing else, she walked away from the village – wandering from town to town in search of her son, carrying only a small bag filled with toys. Praying for a glimpse of him, she walked until her old age, living on charity and scrapings from hotel kitchens, and calling his name, *Aroldo, Aroldo,* as she passed through strange towns, cities and villages.

Aroldo hid his hands in gloves or underneath long sleeves, but he always knew they were the way they were, even if nobody else did. He was too shy to talk to women, and never so much as approached one with romantic intent. He knew they wouldn't want to hold his hand, and that they would never kiss a man whose nose was so purple and so misshapen. He drifted from town to town and from job to job, until one day he found himself minding the pumps at a small filling station on a lonely stretch of road. Five minutes into his first morning's work he decided he would stay there for the rest of his life. It was poorly paid but the work was steady, and the older he grew the less he cared about what people thought of him, and what they thought of his hands and his nose.

He grabbed the nozzle and stuck it in the pick-up's pipe. With his finger he pulled the trigger, until the tank was full. The customer, a foreigner, stared at Aroldo's hands, noticing that as soon as he had replaced the pump, they disappeared under his long shirtsleeves. The foreigner put the money not into a waiting hand, but on to the end of a covered arm. Aroldo took the money without a word. The customer thanked him in bad Italian, got back in and drove away.

'Did you see his hands?' Cockroft asked the Bosnian, who was hiding under his hat and behind his dark glasses.

'No.'

'He only had one finger.'

The Bosnian said nothing.

'Extraordinary.'

Timoleon Vieta peered into the cab through

the dirty back window, his whines escalating into snarls.

Cockroft found somewhere to park in Gubbio, and they walked through winding streets until they reached the Palazzo dei Consoli. 'This town is full of history,' he said. 'It oozes the past. But that's Italy for you. All you have to do is open your eyes, and there's history – staring you in the face.' There were crowds everywhere, lining the streets. 'Today is the Widows Parade,' he explained to his companion. 'It happens every year.'

'Widows? You mean the women who are having the dead husbands?'

'Precisely. It all started hundreds of years ago. Once a year all the widows of Gubbio were made to wear black clothes and walk very slowly through the streets. Then everyone who wasn't a widow would throw rotten fruit at them.'

'Why?'

'To punish them for having been bad wives. It was considered very bad form to allow your husband to die – you were not a good wife, and deserved to be humiliated in front of everyone. They had failed in their duty.'

'But we have no fruit.'

'Oh, my dear boy – they don't throw fruit any more. They haven't for a long time. No, these days everyone simply politely applauds as they pass. We celebrate them, we don't despise them. Times have changed a little. But still, absolutely every widow in Gubbio must attend the parade. I think it's the law.' Usually, when the old man opened his mouth all the Bosnian heard was something like the sound of a waterfall, but for the first time he found himself half interested in what he was saying. He was almost glad to be in Gubbio. He wanted to see these women with dead husbands. It would make a change.

After a while a brass band came along, playing a mournful tune. They were followed by the first of the women. They were dressed in widows' weeds, and were all crying. They clutched black handkerchiefs.

'They have to cry,' explained Cockroft, in a whisper. 'Even today, not crying is seen as a

sign of not having loved your husband enough.'
Everyone in the crowd was clapping very quietly
as they passed.

The procession seemed to go on forever. Some
of the women were simply shaking their heads
and drying their eyes, while others moaned and
sobbed. Towards the end of the line came the
very old women – ones who had difficulty keeping
up. They walked with sticks, their legs bowed and
their backs hunched. The parade ended with a
horse-drawn cart carrying the women whose legs
had given up entirely.

'They're all heading towards the old Roman
amphitheatre,' whispered Cockroft. 'There's always
a big show there. I managed to get a ticket for it
a few years ago, when Spandau Ballet was the star
attraction. You know, the pop group. They weren't
really up my street though – too much saxophone.
I left before the end. The widows get in free of
course, but they aren't supposed to enjoy it. It's
always on television – you can watch it when we
get back if you want to.'

Among the stragglers walked a widow who

was clearly much younger than those around her. Her black clothes looked brand new, and very stylish. As she shuffled past the men, she took her big black handkerchief away from her face. The Bosnian saw that she must only have been about nineteen. She was distraught. Tears were rolling from her big brown eyes, and down her faultless olive cheeks. She was as pretty as a china doll. He heard murmurs from the crowd, and could make out people saying: *Yesterday. It was only yesterday. The poor child.* The Bosnian couldn't remember ever having seen a girl as pretty as this widow, not even in a photograph. He took off his dark glasses so he could see her more clearly. Her hair was tied in a single plait, and hung the length of her back. Suddenly all he wanted in the world was to wipe away her tears with his penis.

When the women had disappeared from view the men found a bar and sat outside, drinking beer and smoking. Cockroft threw pretzels to the dog. The Bosnian couldn't get the young widow out of his mind. He thought of her husband who in his final moments, however fleeting they were, must have been overwhelmed with a sense of self-satisfaction. *I may be dying*, he would have thought to himself, *but bloody hell – look at what I got to fuck while I was alive.* Maybe he had even planted his seed. Maybe he lived on inside her. It would be a boy, and she would name him after his father. As he grew up, his features would resemble his father's more and more, and her love for the child would grow wilder every day. Her new husband would not be blind to this, and would hate the boy with all his heart for forcing him to realise that his wife would never truly love him.

He couldn't help comparing himself to the dead man. He looked at what he had in his own life – a stupid old man who fed him with very ordinary food, bought him cheap clothes and cheap cigarettes, and gave him somewhere half comfortable to stay in exchange for a few minutes of mild displeasure once a week, and a dog he hated and who hated him. It was, he thought, less than nothing. He wondered, not for the first time, whether he should have died long ago. He wondered whether he should have died like the widow's husband, when life was sweet.

Cockroft paid for their beers, and they walked back to the pick-up. Timoleon Vieta scrabbled at the passenger door. 'Oh Timoleon Vieta, really,' said Cockroft. 'You know full well you're going in the back today. We've got a visitor, remember?' He dragged the reluctant dog to the back, and released the flap. Timoleon Vieta started to whine.

Sick of everything, but particularly sick of the sound of the dog's complaining, the Bosnian walked towards him and kicked him hard in his belly. He felt his boot connect with some bone or other. Cockroft couldn't believe it. 'You kicked him.' He was beside himself. 'You kicked Timoleon Vieta.'

'I'm sick of his fucking crap. You treat him like a fucking baby. You should teach him to shut the fuck up. Let's go.'

Winded, the dog gave up his struggle, and allowed his master to tie him up in the back. They got in the cab, and Cockroft drove home without a word. He was angry with the Bosnian for having kicked the dog, angry with Timoleon Vieta for having spoiled what should have been a lovely outing with his misbehaviour, and angry with himself for reasons that he couldn't quite work out.

BORED

By his fourth Wednesday at his new home the Bosnian had more or less got the hang of paying his rent. He entertained the old man for as long as it took, then quickly went downstairs where he drank a pint of water, ate half a packet of strong mints, drank another pint of water, ate the rest of the mints, had a slug of whiskey straight from the bottle and lit a cigarette. On the third week he had tried drinking a bottle of beer instead of the whiskey, but the gas had brought the taste back into his mouth. He didn't enjoy the experience, but he wasn't disgusted by it either. He just did it. It wasn't much different from being with a girl who he would never have looked at if she hadn't had a hotel room to share, and he had done that enough times since he had been in Italy. It was easy. It was boring.

As he waited for the old man to come back downstairs and start cooking their meal, it struck him that all the time he had been at the house he had never known the telephone to ring or any letters to arrive. He was certain nobody had dropped by.

But, two days later, the postman called. Cockroft knew who the letter was from before he even opened it. It was from his accountant. She occasionally justified her fee by gleefully reminding him how little money he had, or telling him how well various stocks and shares that he had chosen not to buy were doing. He owned small chunks of British Telecom, Marks and Spencer, David Bowie, and something like a bauxite mine in the Polders or somewhere, and she told him about them too. He opened the letter at the breakfast table, and read it aloud.

'I am very sorry to have to inform you,' he read, 'that hundreds of thousands of students whose minds have become addled by the overuse of illicit recreational substances have become drawn to your pathetic *Bibbly And The Bobblies* puppet show. The wankers at BBC2 are repeating every fucking one of them at six o'clock on Tuesday evenings (when these future captains of our once proud nation should be watching the news) and ten-thirty on Sunday mornings (when the useless cunts stagger in from a night out on crack cocaine and ecstasy and are too stupid to realise that they saw the poxy programme the Tuesday before, not that it makes any difference because each episode is exactly the fucking same as the next as far as I can tell). Anyway, it's going to be an undeservedly good year for you. First payment, £6,200, due to land in your account in 6-8 weeks, and more to follow as and when. Video compilation in shops for Christmas. Your name off credits naturally. I don't know what the fucking world's coming to. Yours subserviently . . .'

'Oh,' said the old man. 'This is wonderful news.'

'I did not understand,' said the Bosnian.

'I'm so sorry. I'm a little over excited.' He

explained, slowly. 'A long time ago, in the early nineteen seventies, I wrote the music for a children's television programme called *Bibbly And The Bobblies*. It was about some puppets on the moon or somewhere, and was full of flashing, swirling colours, because colour television was new then and the people who made the programmes didn't know when to stop. Now, young people, students mainly, who smoke drugs and enjoy looking at lots of different colours at the same time, have started to watch it. The television people in England, that's my country, are showing them all again, and I will be getting some money.'

Cockroft's royalties usually trickled in very slowly, and this kind of unexpected windfall hadn't happened to him for some time. Four years earlier the Japanese group *My Sweetheart Sensation* had used a part of one of his tunes on their album, and a while after that an American singer whose name escaped him had, for some reason, used a melody from one of his songs for the chorus of a lacklustre teen-sex anthem called *We Might As Well Be Married (If You Think About It)*. It had reached number fifty-four. These had made him a few thousand pounds. Tax bills and commission had absorbed almost all of the money, and the change had gone on weekends away and treats for himself and the dog. He was particularly pleased with his new windfall because he had come up with all the incidental music for *Bibbly And The Bobblies* by tape recording his farts and belches, and the drops of urine that trickled into the lavatory pan as he shook his penis dry. He had written these sounds in musical notation for oboe, double bass and glockenspiel, and sold them to the BBC. For months, when strangers had asked him what he did for a living, he had told them, 'Burping, farting, and pissing in the toilet.' They rarely knew what to say.

The Bosnian had always admired and understood pretty girls with rich boyfriends, particularly when they befriended penniless Bosnians when nobody was looking, which had happened twice. He started thinking about what he could get from the old man.

'So, you are a rich man's plaything,' said Cockroft, as if reading his mind. 'How do you like that?'

The Bosnian didn't say anything. He remembered *Bibbly And The Bobblies*, but couldn't remember how the music went.

Cockroft decided to mark the good news with a celebratory trip to the supermarket.

'To make this day very special,' said the Bosnian, 'we must be leaving your dog here.'

Cockroft, in his elation, agreed, telling himself that they would not be gone for much more than a couple of hours, and that Timoleon Vieta would appreciate some time alone in the house. He would be able to gather his thoughts. So the two men drove away, leaving the dog behind.

The old man was determined to fill the trolley, and anything that looked nice went into it. Sauces, spices, deodorants, frozen meat, frozen fish, fresh vegetables, pasta, wine, brandy, whiskey, a new frying pan, biscuits, seven bottles of champagne and lots of cigars and cigarettes. He came across the pet section, and was delighted. He bought a dozen chewy bones, a pair of bouncy balls, some catnip to see if it had the same effect on dogs as it did on cats, and the most expensive lead on the rack.

When they got back to the house Cockroft threw a chewy bone to Timoleon Vieta and started cooking an enormous lunch. While they were eating, the old man suggested they go for a walk when they finished. Even though the dog seemed to have become increasingly standoffish and grumpy, choosing to spend as much time as he could on his own, Cockroft was still feeling guilty about having left him to his own devices while they had been at the shops. He felt as though he should take at least some of the blame for the rift that was appearing between them, and do whatever he could to mend it. 'What do you say? Just you, me and Timoleon Vieta. The three musketeers.'

The Bosnian shrugged. 'I don't care.'

The walk took them up the hill, along the track

and a long way into the woods. They didn't talk much. Cockroft sometimes hummed a fragment of an overture, Timoleon Vieta went on ahead and the Bosnian did his best to lag behind. When they reached a point with a view the men stopped, sat on the ground and looked into the distance as the dog sniffed around a short way away. Both men, full of food and champagne, lay back and fell asleep.

Cockroft was the first to wake up, and he noticed straight away that Timoleon Vieta was not with them. He panicked. 'Wake up,' he said. 'Quickly, we've got to find Timoleon Vieta. Get up.'

The Bosnian rubbed his eyes and slowly rose to his feet. He thought it was nice without the dog around. The old man was in a frenzy, but things still seemed strangely peaceful. He hoped the dog would never be found.

'Timoleon Vieta. Timoleon Vieta, come here.' The old man was shouting, his hands cupped around his mouth. 'Oh my God,' he muttered to himself. 'Timoleon Vieta, how could I have fallen asleep? This is all my fault. It's always my fault.' He couldn't even think of the last time he had seen him. He began to hurry back the way they had come, calling all the way. The dog did not appear.

The Bosnian hated situations like this. He followed at a distance, yawning and rubbing his eyes.

At every bend Cockroft prayed for the dog to come bounding towards him, his tail wagging and his tongue lolling from his mouth, just like in the old days. But bend followed bend, and there was no dog to be seen. 'Why, Timoleon Vieta? Why?' he cried. 'Why did you have to run away from me?'

They reached the house. Cockroft was sweating. He was short of breath, and had turned red. He kept calling until he saw, slumped on the doorstep, Timoleon Vieta. He ran to him, and fell on him. He embraced him. 'Oh Timoleon Vieta, I thought you were gone forever. You gave me the fright of my life. Why do you have to be so naughty, Timoleon Vieta? What have I done to deserve this?'

The Bosnian let himself in, stepping around the emotional reunion. He was very tired of the saga of the man and his dog. The only thing he wanted was to spend some time being bored, not having to think about anything. The man and the dog were almost unbelievably boring, but they were the wrong kind of boring. The kind of boredom he craved was one without a tedious drama in front of him every time he opened his eyes. But then, he thought, if one or other of the players stopped being around, he could start being really, really bored.

That evening Cockroft and the Bosnian sat in the deckchairs in front of the house, drinking more champagne and looking out at the old farm houses that were dotted around the hills. Cockroft's distant neighbours' homes disappeared or became tiny spots of light as it grew dark. He knew a lot of the people who lived in those places, though he rarely saw them any more. Most of them were English, and like him had come to Umbria to start a new life, to try to escape from whatever it was that had been wrong with their old lives. A lot of them were writing books about themselves

and their little Italian houses. In the days before
he had slipped off the bottom of their invitation
lists he had been given a stream of manuscripts
to look at and comment on. At first he had read
them thoroughly. They were all more or less the
same, with very similar anecdotes about botched
DIY and meetings with their obliviously comical
Italian neighbours, many of them pock-marked,
and at first he had given them back saying simply,
'It's very good indeed. Really super.' The authors
were never quite happy with this, and always asked
him whether or not their books were witty, and
whether they had successfully evoked the many
scents of Umbria. In the end he gave up reading
them. He would keep the manuscript for a week
before giving it back, saying, 'It's very good indeed.
Really super. It's *very* witty, and you evoke the
many scents of Umbria *so* well.' For a while he
had quite a reputation as a literary critic. On trips
back to England he visited bookshops, and each
time he saw more of these books on the shelves,
recognising a fair few of the authors' names. Books
with titles like *Olive Oil And Sunset: An Umbrian*

Odyssey, or *Uffizi Lover: A Year of Bruschetta and Botticelli*, or *Cracked Walls and Chianti: Five Seasons on a Tuscan Hillside*, all of which carried the same subtext: *Oh, we bought a charming little house in the Italian countryside.* Each time he went back he expected the bubble to have burst, but they kept on appearing on the shelves.

After one such visit Cockroft had decided to jump on the bandwagon. He looked out for incidents he could turn into witty anecdotes, but nothing interesting ever seemed to happen to him. Like all his neighbours he tried hard to evoke the many scents of Umbria, but he soon became bored and anyway he couldn't work out why anybody would want to read about them. All he had completed was a forty-page chapter about a walk he and Timoleon Vieta had taken, during which he had almost trodden on a snake, when he decided not to bother any more.

Trying to write the book had, at least for a while, made him appreciate his humdrum life. He was glad that he could go from day to day with very little happening to him. It certainly beat having things that were worth writing about happening to him all the time.

Sometimes he would bump into the people who lived in those houses when he was shopping in town and he would pass the time of day, but he only socialised with them every once in a while. He didn't mind this. He was tired of their conversation. They talked endlessly about how they had left England because it was becoming swamped by foreigners or being run by pro-European Stalinists, about how untrustworthy the Italians were, how expensive they had found everything on their trips back to England, and about the best places to buy olive oil.

'I tried to write a book about this place once,' Cockroft said to the Bosnian.

The Bosnian said nothing in return.

The sky filled with clouds, and they heard a rumble of thunder in the distance. 'It looks as though summer's here,' said Cockroft, rolling his eyes. Timoleon Vieta dashed inside. Spots of rain began to fall, and the men followed him. Cockroft sat at the kitchen table, and the Bosnian went to his room. He found his knife. It was in his bag, inside a sock. He took his small whetstone and with the storm growing louder and muffling the sound, he sharpened the already sharp six-inch blade as the lights flickered on and off, not quite in time with the flashes and the roars.

DUMPED

The boy in the silver shorts had been a joy to look at and to kiss. In the four months they had spent together he had given Cockroft a reason to stay alive. He had, despite his tender years, acquired the most delicious repertoire of ways in which to manipulate an old man's mind and body into a beautiful delirium. He and Timoleon Vieta had found themselves soul mates, and until its sudden, unhappy end the whole affair had been a honeymoon. But the boy in the silver shorts could not do DIY. He could recline like Cleopatra on her barge, but he couldn't even change a light bulb.

Taking his time about it, and trying his hardest not to think about it, the Bosnian had stripped and painted all the window frames on the front of the house. His mother had always forced him to do jobs around the house in his school holidays, saying that a man wasn't a real man unless he could handle tools, and that it would do him good to understand what it meant to do a hard day's work, so he knew what he had to do and roughly how to go about it. When it had suited him he had demonstrated his DIY skills to single girls who wanted new shelves, or who needed small plastering jobs done. He had always known he would be rewarded very well as they gave full rein to their handyman daydreams.

The work he had done on the house had been nothing more than a way of keeping him slightly occupied in a way that kept him fit. He was surprised at how much of a difference it made, and he even found himself feeling almost proud of his work. 'Look at your new house,' he said to the old man, seeing him through an open window. Cockroft came out, and there by his heels was Timoleon Vieta.

'Oh, how lovely. What do you think, Timoleon

Vieta? Doesn't the house look smart?' Timoleon Vieta sniffed a pile of animal droppings.

In this unexpected moment of near-satisfaction, the Bosnian suddenly felt a pang of affection for the dog. It took him by surprise. He looked at Timoleon Vieta, and instead of an enemy he saw an ordinary dog. Just another mongrel. He approached him, saying, 'So the windows do not interest you, dog?' He reached out to pat the animal's head and scratch behind his ears in the way dogs seem to enjoy. Timoleon Vieta growled, and sank his teeth into the Bosnian's hand, drawing blood. The Bosnian kicked the dog away, his boot smashing hard into the side of Timoleon Vieta's head. 'Fucking dog cunt,' he said.

'Oh, Timoleon Vieta,' said Cockroft. 'Really.'

The Bosnian went into the kitchen and started washing his hand. Cockroft followed him. The atmosphere was fraught.

'Your dog it does not like me,' mumbled the young man.

'Oh, he does. He thinks you're super.'

'What?'

Cockroft sighed. 'Well, I suppose he's just a bit difficult to get to know, and once you get to know him a little better you'll be best of friends. You wait and see.'

'But maybe I do not want to know your fucking stupid fucking dog. Maybe I do not want to be friends with your fucking dog. Maybe I hate him very much. Maybe I am wishing he was not around.'

Cockroft desperately wanted the man and the dog to get along. It was important to him. Sometimes, when he thought of them both, he thought of them as *my boys*. 'He's lovely really. I'm sure you'll be friends in the end. Just give it time.'

They went to their rooms to lie down. The Bosnian fell asleep straight away, but Cockroft was troubled. He thought about what the Bosnian had said about hating Timoleon Vieta. It seemed as though the visitor had brought out the worst in the dog – he had had bad moods and fits of growling before, and he had not always made friends with people who had come to stay, but he had never been so relentlessly hostile to anyone. *It's almost as though he's become a different dog altogether*, he thought to himself. *It's as if we're drifting apart. Sometimes I wonder whether I really know him any more.* He thought of the preceding weeks. Timoleon Vieta had spent even more time than usual away from the house, and when he returned he was always in a strange mood. It just wasn't like him, thought Cockroft. He had been so surly, and he had made no effort at all to welcome the Bosnian.

Cockroft thought back to some of the times he had spent living alone, and how much he had hated it. It was as if there were two different versions of him, one of which only came alive when there was another person around. When he lived alone he drank alone, and that always stopped when he had a visitor to drink with. When he lived alone he would spend whole days crying, but he never did that when there was somebody else there, and he would go for days on end without having a bath, but he always washed regularly if there was somebody around to smell him. When he lived alone he used toenail clippings and pubic hairs as bookmarks, and talked to himself, the one musketeer, almost all the time. There didn't even have to be romance in the air for his visitor to be lavished with food, comfort, attention and love. Once an eighteen-year-old girl, a niece of his dear dead friend Robin 'Red Breast' Robinson, had sought him out and stayed with him in the summer before starting university. He had loved having her around. After he found her lying on the kitchen floor, smearing dog food on to her nipples and having it licked off by the rough tongue of the Dalmatian, he had told her she wasn't to feel embarrassed and that she was more than welcome to stay, but she had packed and left, in floods of tears. There were weeks to go before she had to be at college, but she wouldn't stay. She begged Cockroft not to tell anyone, and he never did.

Despite his motto, *You're never alone with internal dialogue,* he was desperate not to live on his own again, and for the first time he found himself thinking that maybe things would be better if Timoleon Vieta was not around. He was horrified by these thoughts and tried to drive them out of his mind, but no matter how far he tried to drive them they kept on coming back.

The Bosnian decided that he had to choose between killing the dog, secretly so the old man would never find out, or just packing up and leaving. Staying in the same house as it was not an option. He thought that if he killed it and dumped it in the woods, the old man's distress at its disappearance would be even more irritating than the animal itself.

He decided to leave that night, while the old man was sleeping. Disappearing had always been his favourite way of leaving a place. He thought there was something poetic about it. It was how he had left his country, and how he had left most of the girls he had known since he had been in Italy. He would quietly unzip the tent just before dawn and vanish, maybe taking her money with him so he could catch a bus to another town with another campsite, where he would find another girl to impress with the scar from his bullet wound. He always liked to imagine the look on the face of the girl he had left as she woke up to find he wasn't there beside her, as the realisation dawned that her Bosnian wasn't in the shower or getting breakfast ready on the stove. She was always crying her eyes out.

But, thinking about it, he decided he might as well wait until breakfast the next morning and leave then. He might even be able to get a lift to the bus station, with a full belly and hours of daylight in front of him.

At the breakfast table Cockroft implored him to stay. 'You can't expect me to drive you to the bus station. I can't. Stay. Please. Stay and keep me company.' He saw the future stretched before him, a desert of loneliness. 'We'll have such fun.'

After another comfortable night in the guest bedroom and an enormous breakfast, and with the prospect of yet another day with nothing much to do, the Bosnian was beginning to wonder whether he couldn't wait a while before leaving. 'I would be staying here,' he mumbled. 'But it is that fucking dog already. I hate that dog and that dog hates me. He goes or I go. We cannot be sharing one house.'

'I'm so sorry,' Cockroft said. 'We've got to find a solution. I'm sure we can.'

'If that dog bite me once more I will kill it. Of course I will kill it – it is my instinct.'

'Oh, you couldn't – he's just a dumb animal.'

'It is nature. He attack me and he will die,' he said, miming a karate chop. 'I am from Bosnia, and in Bosnia we are killing the dogs all the time with only our hands.' Again, he mimed a karate chop.

'Oh no. You can't do that.'

They stopped talking. The weather forecast was on the radio.

'But I am having a good idea,' said the Bosnian, after a while. 'One to keep us, you and me, happy.'

'What is it?'

'Easy. I will kill the dog right now. Because if I am staying here he will be biting me, right? And when he bite me I kill him, right? So I kill him right now. I have killed many dogs already. I don't know how many, I lose the count, but a lot of. It is easy. In Bosnia we learn about it in school.' Cockroft was speechless. 'You snap the dog's neck in one simple movement, or grab the dog at back of dog's neck and hit it on the front of the neck a couple of times,' he tapped his own throat with his clenched fist. 'Maybe three times or four times. Then they die. It is very fast. They feel nothing. I think maybe they even enjoy it.'

'But you can't kill Timoleon Vieta. He's . . .' Cockroft almost said that Timoleon Vieta was his best friend. 'He's my dog.'

'Do not worry. It will be quick and I will dig the hole for him in the ground. I will make a wooden cross like at the church. It will be giving me something to do. I think he will be happy down there.'

Cockroft was close to tears at the thought of Timoleon Vieta's violent death. 'Couldn't we just muzzle him?' He made a muzzle out of his hand, clamping his own face to illustrate his suggestion. 'Put a cage thing on his face?'

'No. He will still be here. He will still make the noises and he will attack me with his nose and his, I don't know, his hands, and if he attack me he die. Remember,' said the Bosnian, who had never even been to Bosnia, and who wasn't sure he would be able to find it on a map, 'I am from Bosnia.'

The thought of living alone frightened Cockroft as much as it always did before it happened, but he loved Timoleon Vieta to distraction even though the dog seemed to have gone cool on him. His head swam. 'Please stay. I'm sure you two will become friends in time.'

'No. We will not be being good friends.' The Bosnian had learned never to make friends with anyone, or anything, who had once been his adversary. A reconciliation was out of the question. 'But I am having one more idea.'

'What is it?'

'The dog is the wild animal already, right? You tell me he was the wild animal when he arrive to you. He is knowing how to be surviving on his own, right? It is simple. We take him away. We leave him someplace else. He is happy being the wild animal again, and we live with the peace right here. Maybe,' he said, putting his hand on Cockroft's shoulder, 'with the peace, you and me we are becoming very good friends.'

Cockroft enjoyed the sensation of the Bosnian's hand on his shoulder. It wasn't quite like a dream, but he enjoyed it nonetheless. 'Oh, but it all sounds too barbaric.' He shivered at the thought of Timoleon Vieta all alone in the world.

'Then shall I be killing the dog?' The Bosnian withdrew his hand. 'Or shall I be walking to the bus?'

'No.' Cockroft stood up. 'Please. Let me think about it for a while. Give me a day to decide. Please.' He poured himself a brandy in a wine glass.

By half past ten Cockroft was so drunk he could hardly see. By eleven he had staggered to his room and fallen asleep, the curtains open and light pouring on to his face. When he woke up at three o'clock in the afternoon he started drinking again. Timoleon Vieta drifted in and out of the house as though it were just an ordinary day, and Cockroft drifted in and out of consciousness. In the late afternoon he was shaken awake by the Bosnian, and without knowing what he was doing, followed his orders. He put Timoleon Vieta on his lead and tied him up in the back of the pick-up.

'Give me the keys,' said the Bosnian.

'Why? Where are you going?'

'I am going now to be dumping the dog like we agreed already.' He knew the old man was so drunk that he hardly knew what was going on. And besides, he felt like going on a long drive.

Cockroft burst into tears. 'Did I agree to that?' He really didn't know. 'I'm coming with you,' he slurred. 'You're not going without me. I'm coming to say goodbye.'

The Bosnian had known the old man would say that, and anyway he would probably need him there to pay for fuel. 'OK. You come. But bring money. And I drive.'

Cockroft staggered inside the house, then came back out with a half-bottle of Scotch. He locked the door of the house and walked over to the pick-up, where Timoleon Vieta was wailing in the back and the Bosnian was in the driving seat, ready to go.

'Where are you taking him?' asked Cockroft.

'I do not know. But it will be a long way from here.'

'Go to Rome,' said Cockroft. 'He'll love it in Rome. All those cats to chase. He'll have the time of his life.' He got into the pick-up. 'We've got to leave him somewhere nice.' He thought of the places he liked in Rome. There were plenty of them, but one eclipsed all its competitors. 'Let's leave him at the Wedding Cake,' he said. Cockroft always preferred to call the Vittorio Emanuele Monument by its nickname. It was, by a long way, his favourite building in the world – a huge, fancy slab of marble with eternal flames and fountains, a dead soldier somewhere inside it and horses poised on top, four on each side, looking as if they were about to leap into the heavens. He had often sat outside a bar across the piazza from it, drinking beer, admiring the green lasers shining from its roof, mumbling to himself about the juxtaposition of ancient and modern, and wishing he was dead. He would picture himself in a thunderstorm, sitting on top of one of the horses on the left-hand side, shouting something from *King Lear* (which he kept meaning to re-read, because the only line he could remember was *Out, vile jelly*) before jumping off, his blood smearing the greying white marble, mixing with the rainwater and running like pink champagne towards the drains while his soul soared with the horses into eternity.

He had never quite got around to devising a way of getting past the guards and up on to a horse, and as he thought about it he decided the Wedding Cake wouldn't be right for Timoleon Vieta. 'No,' he said. 'Let's leave him at the Colosseum. Yes. The Colosseum. I love the Colosseum. It's why I came to this country in the first place. I kept seeing pictures of it. With all its . . . bricks. He'll be so much happier there.' Cockroft thought the Colosseum was somehow more historically significant than the Vittorio Emanuele Monument, and Timoleon Vieta was historically significant too, so it would be appropriate. They had been through a lot together over the years. It seemed to make sense. And besides, he remembered having seen some cats playing there, and Timoleon Vieta would enjoy chasing them, and he could even eat them if he wanted to because there wouldn't be anyone to stop him.

The Bosnian hadn't been behind a wheel for a long time, and liked the idea of a long drive. 'OK. We go to Roma.'

Cockroft spent the journey drinking, sleeping, crying, and proclaiming his joy at the thought of Timoleon Vieta's fresh start in life. He seemed oblivious to the Bosnian's dangerous driving, as he pushed the pick-up to its limit, the bumper just inches from the car in front. 'I've been holding him back all these years,' the old man said. 'He'll have such a wonderful time.' He couldn't bring himself to look through the back window at the dog who, every time the Bosnian swerved or braked sharply, was thrown around, his collar pulling tight around his throat.

It was getting dark by the time they pulled into the bus stop in front of the Colosseum. Cockroft had imagined himself plunging from the highest wall of the Colosseum too, quietly and nakedly falling at the dead of night. He had pictured his body lying

116

unnoticed by passers-by, and being picked to pieces by bats like flying piranhas until nothing was left of him but a skeleton. Two people were standing there, waiting for a bus. They didn't seem to be at all interested in the pick-up, or the historical significance of the location. The old man did as he was told and got out, climbed up into the back and untied Timoleon Vieta. The Bosnian retreated a short way, and watched as the old man led his pet down to the pavement. The dog's tail was between his legs. Cockroft hugged him, and kissed his head. 'Goodbye Timoleon Vieta,' he whispered. 'Goodbye, and thank you so much for everything.' He wished he had taken his camera. 'I love you, Timoleon Vieta. Never forget that. Please understand why I'm doing this. I couldn't bear to be alone again. And I wouldn't be leaving you if I didn't think you would be fine here. There's always lots of food on the ground, and there'll be other dogs to play with and cats to chase. You'll have the time of your life here, won't you? It'll be just like the old days again, before I came along and ruined your fun. And anyway,' said Cockroft, raising his voice, 'it's what you wanted isn't it? You're just the same as all the others, aren't you? You all get sick of me in the end. You all fall out of love with me, if you ever even loved me at all, which I don't suppose you did.' Everybody who had ever told Cockroft that they loved him had subsequently gone out of their way to retract it. Everybody, that is, apart from the boy in the silver shorts, who had simply left him in the middle of the night, when he had been passed out drunk, leaving a one word note (*SORRY!!!*) and never getting back in touch. He was fairly sure the boy was still around though. He had heard stories about him, one of which, from some time before, had him engaged to Monty 'Misty' Moore. They were said to have been planning a big wedding by his pool. He assumed it had all gone ahead. 'You all get tired of me, don't you?'

It had become just another break up and, as much as he wanted Timoleon Vieta to stay, he knew that the dog's future lay elsewhere.

A policeman emerged from the shadow of the Colosseum, about a hundred yards away. He was looking towards the awkwardly parked pick-up.

'Let's go,' said the Bosnian, walking towards them. The old man didn't seem to hear. He just carried on stroking the dog's head and whispering to him. The Bosnian quickly unbuckled the dog's collar, and bundled the old man over to the passenger door. 'Police,' he said. He got in and drove.

PART TWO

Timoleon Vieta Come Home

ABBONDIO

Cosimo watched the pick-up drive away. He was desperate to get home to his wife, and didn't want to get caught up with the kind of people who would abandon a dog at a bus stop. Not wanting to involve himself with unpleasant people had been a problem for him ever since he had joined the police. The idea of being a policeman had never crossed his mind until his then fiancée's father, a senior officer, had started pressurising him into signing up. Wild with love for the girl, Cosimo had told himself that it would be for the best, and that everything would somehow work out in the long run. He had hated it for fifteen years, and what he hated most of all was having to come face to face with the kind of people who were so horrible that they would think nothing of leaving a dog all alone in the world. Still, he thought, the dog would be better off without them. If he had stopped the pick-up and made the men take the dog away, they would only have driven it to a dark place and slit its throat.

But he couldn't just leave it there. Most of his colleagues would have done. They tormented him for his gentle nature and his hopelessness as a police officer. They made comments about the way he was almost always confined to administrative work, and was only ever sent out of the station to perform the most routine tasks, like walking around the Colosseum to check for beggars and to tell bare-chested tourists to put their t-shirts back on. They sat under trees in the park, talking in groups about how much more manly they were than him. They would have considered the rounding up of a stray dog to have been beneath them, and would have gone out of their way to make sure they failed to notice the whole incident, but Cosimo's heart burned with pity for the animal.

He walked towards it, and as he did he noticed its eyes – they were the loveliest, most worried eyes he had ever seen on a dog. They reminded him of the pictures his wife painted. It was a shared love of plants and animals that had brought them together when they were at college, and they had never stopped trying out new ways of attracting birds and butterflies to the tiny garden at the back of their ground floor apartment, and they often drove out into the countryside, where they would spend hours on end looking at things through binoculars. She sold paintings of flowers, trees and birds to shops, and occasionally somebody would ask her to paint their pet cat or dog. She always drew them, even the nastiest ones, with their heads tilted to one side and with oversized, yearning eyes that would tug the heartstrings of their owners. The money wasn't much, but she enjoyed it. Every time she came home after having painted somebody else's pet, she told her husband how she longed for an animal of her own. A cat or a dog, she didn't mind. But then, after thinking about it for a while, she always came down in favour of a dog, because a cat would be much more likely to catch butterflies and to scare the birds away from their garden. He said that they should wait until they'd had a baby before getting a pet, in case the animal turned out to be aggressive towards the newcomer, and she always agreed in the end. It was a conversation they had had many times.

But this dog was irresistible, and he decided to take it home with him. *There's someone here to see you*, he would call, before leading it into the apartment. He imagined his wife's face lighting up at the sight of their new pet. They would call him Abbondio. His wife would paint his picture, and hang it in the hallway.

He crouched, held out a hand to the dog, and gestured for him to approach. 'Come here,' he called, patting his thigh, his forearm brushing against his holster. 'Come here, Abbondio.' The dog backed away. 'Come and say hello.' Slowly, and still crouching, Cosimo moved forward, and Abbondio ran across the road, as fast as he could. Cosimo was helpless as the dog shot away. 'Goodbye Abbondio,' he said, as the dog was almost crushed by an empty coach. On reaching the other side Abbondio disappeared, running down Via Dei Fori Imperiali and out of the policeman's sight.

Cosimo started walking back to the police station. He wondered whether he should tell his wife about what had happened. Maybe he would tell her about seeing the dog being abandoned, then he would describe him, his coat and his sad, beautiful eyes, and tell her about his plan to bring him home and for them to keep him as a pet, and about how he had run away so fast that there was no hope of ever catching up with him. She would smile at the story, and he would smile as he told it. 'Never mind,' one or other of them would say. 'After all, it was only a dog.' And after dinner they would watch some television, play cards and look through books and magazines about plants and animals until they had difficulty keeping their eyes open and had to go to bed.

The two men drove out of the city in silence. Travelling back from Rome with a crippling sense of loss was nothing new for Cockroft. He had driven enough men and boys to the airport and left them near passport control, unable to kiss them goodbye and knowing he would never see them again. He had returned home empty-handed after weekends of trawling the bars looking for a replacement housemate. He had driven back with the boy in the silver shorts after weekends in the city, when they had walked around the galleries and the ruins, and stolen furtive kisses in the Catacombs. Even the happy memories were sad.

'You know, I don't think you're insured,' said Cockroft, slapping the dashboard. He drained the last of the whiskey, and fell asleep.

I'd be very happy to accept something from Compassion

TEG

The girl had a five pound coin in her hand. She wasn't wearing a coat, and a warm, gentle shower was dampening her clothes, but she hardly noticed and she didn't care. Since she had found out about it she had daydreamed of her visit to this spot. She had read that visitors to the city who throw a coin into the water are sure to return, and she had spent the autumn, the winter and the early part of the spring imagining her and Enrico standing there on their last night together, before she had to get the plane to Cardiff where her dad or her brother would be waiting to pick her up and take her back home. She had dreamed of Enrico putting his arms around her, kissing her and begging her to come back for good as soon as she could, to live in Rome and perhaps even to marry him. She hadn't pictured herself standing there on her own, wondering what to do with the coin she had brought over specially.

She had spent the summer before in Tenby, working seven days a week in a shop on a caravan site to save money to take to college. Enrico had been spending a few weeks in the town, working in a cafe run by some distant relatives. A student, he had been practising his English by telling girls how beautiful they were. Sometimes they teased him by speaking Welsh, and pretending they couldn't understand English at all. She had fallen in love with him the moment he sat at her table and asked, politely, whether she would mind talking to him for a while. They spent the last weeks of the summer together, Enrico creeping away from her tiny caravan in the early hours of the morning and going back to the cafe to start work. When he had to go back to Rome, they parted with promises and extravagant words of love.

She deferred her place at college, found a job in

a shop near her parents' home, saved money and learned as much Italian as she could from books and tapes. She sent Enrico a book on how to speak Welsh. She told him it wasn't that important because everyone she knew spoke English too, but that she hoped he would remember just a few words because her family would appreciate it when he came to meet them. They would certainly find it funny. He wrote back saying he would learn as much as he could. They arranged to meet in Rome for a month in the spring, to see how well they got along outside Tenby, and to see what she thought of his city. She knew she would fall in love with it, and that she would never be taking up her place at college. She had already started making arrangements for her move to Italy. Her guide book told her she could be an au pair. She didn't mind children too much, so finding a job and somewhere to live wouldn't be that hard. She had also read that she could make a bit of money on the side by helping people with their English. The book didn't say anything about helping people with their Welsh, but there were four million people in Rome so she thought there must be somebody there who wanted to learn.

At last, she arrived at Leonardo da Vinci airport. Enrico was there to meet her. She asked him to speak a bit of Welsh, but he said he couldn't remember anything except *helo, hwyl, iechyd da* and *diolch yn fawr*. They took the train into the city, standing out by the toilets so they didn't have to worry about how much noise they made while they were kissing. They walked from the station to a hotel on Via Firenze. Enrico told her that it would be quicker than queuing for a taxi. He carried her bag. It had been two weeks since he had written to tell her where she would be staying and how they would be getting there, and since then she had followed the route on her map over and over again, imagining what it would be like. The air was thick and warm and unmistakably Italian, and everything was at least ten times better than she had dared to think it would be. The buildings were taller than she had imagined, more perfectly crumbling, and sometimes built in the strangest shapes. With Enrico beside her she felt invincible as they crossed the streets, Fiats and Mercedes missing them by a whisker in both directions. The only thing that didn't take her by surprise was that Rome felt, immediately, like home.

She wasn't used to staying in hotels, so she didn't really know what to expect from the place Enrico had booked her in to. She hadn't expected it to be the way it was. Rather than being a whole building, it was more like somebody's flat. They had to ring a bell and climb three flights of stairs before they got to it. Everything was slightly yellow, and a little girl of about three with curly hair and enormous eyes rode her plastic tricycle up and down behind the reception desk. The place smelled of old people and cooking. She gave a man her passport, and signed her name on a piece of paper. Enrico had arranged a discount for her because she would be staying for such a long time, and she wouldn't be wanting them to make breakfast for her. He told her she could buy cheap bread from a small supermarket not too far away. The place was noisy. As they had sex, she could hear a television in the next room. It was some kind of variety show. It ended, and what sounded like the news came on.

The next day he took her to the Colosseum, to St. Peter's and for a walk along the concrete banks of the Tiber. It was only her second time abroad, and she loved it. She enjoyed the feeling of being lost among rivers of Japanese and Catholic tourists as much as she enjoyed the things they went to see. They went back to the hotel. Later, as they ate dinner in a brightly lit café on a quiet street, she asked him when she was going to get to meet his family, and he told her in a few days time, once she had had a chance to settle in and they had been able to spend some time together, just the two of them. He told her he had missed her, and that he didn't want to share her with anybody for a while. They went to a nightclub, where they danced for a few songs. It was a Tuesday, so it wasn't very full.

On her fourth day in Rome Enrico called her hotel and left a message saying that he wouldn't be able to see her that night, that he would be busy studying. She understood that he needed to work hard to pass his exams, so instead of going out with him she went to the cinema, where she saw a sexual comedy that wasn't very sexy and didn't seem to be very funny. There were seven other people in the audience, and none of them were laughing. She could tell what was happening just by looking at it, but she still listened out for words she could understand. Afterwards she spent a while playing football with the little girl at the hotel, and had an early night.

Enrico had a lot of college work to do, a lot of unexpected essays and presentations, so she spent more time alone than she had expected, living on ruins and supermarket bread. As she walked around, she amused herself by trying to work out who was Italian and who wasn't. She was surprised by how different Italians looked from one another, and felt stupid for feeling so surprised. She had expected all the men to look more or less the same as Enrico, only not quite as handsome, and the girls' dark colouring to make her feel as though her light brown hair were golden, but there were jowly young men in suits with slight builds, paunches and receding hair, and girls whose hair and skin was so fair that she would never have thought they were Italian if she hadn't heard them talk. There were Romans with glasses and Romans with limps, and there was at least one Roman in a wheelchair.

Without Enrico she was wary of crossing the street. Even when the green light said *Avanti* she walked carefully because the roaring cars edged forwards so aggressively. Sometimes she sheltered next to a nun, knowing she would be safe. She wondered about what she would have to do to become a Catholic. She liked the churches and wanted lots of babies, so she didn't think it would be too much of a problem. She supposed she would have to come off the pill at some point. Every old building she passed seemed as though it would be worth visiting. If she saw one she particularly liked the look of but that she couldn't find in her guide book, she would wonder how old it was, and what it was doing there, and whether you had to pay to get in. When she was tired she went back to her room. The hotel was never quiet. The pipes sang, strange noises rumbled from downstairs, the family who ran the place shouted either to each other or at each other all the time, and every time somebody walked through the front door an aggressive buzzer rang. It sounded exactly the same as her alarm clock at home, and it jarred her awake whenever she was about to fall asleep. When she couldn't sleep at all she read her phrase book, or played with the little girl, who was quiet and nice and called Rosita.

Enrico could only ever fit her in at the strangest times, sometimes arranging to meet her from eight in the morning until nine-thirty, or sometimes not being able to turn up until after midnight. When they were together, peeling off each other's clothes, there always seemed to be people walking up and down right outside their room. She almost thought she could hear them breathing, but sometimes she had to cry out, not caring who heard. Even so it wasn't the same as in Tenby, where they had had a caravan to themselves and could forget that anyone else existed, but she was so happy just to be with him that she didn't worry about it too much.

After two weeks, as they lay on the bed in the afternoon, she asked him again when she was going to get to meet his family. He told her that she couldn't ever meet them because they didn't know about her, and that he already had a girlfriend who they liked very much and who he was probably going to marry. He put his hand on her hip, kissed her lips and told her that he thought she was beautiful, and that he loved her small white breasts and light brown hair, but that they had to keep things secret. After a moment's reflection she hit him hard in the face, and pushed him out of the room. Rosita, passing on her tricycle, wept at her first sight of a semi-erect penis. Her tears stopped as she became mesmerised by its changing shape. It drooped and shrank as Enrico banged on the door and asked to be let back in. By the time the door opened a crack and he was hit in the face by a bundle of his own clothes, Rosita was well on the way to being happy again.

When she was sure that Enrico had left the hotel, she got dressed and went to a travel agent, where she was able to book a seat on a flight home the following morning. She went back to the hotel, where she packed her bags and cried. When she had stopped crying she went to the fountain.

She sat right by the water, and rolled the coin around in her hand. 'It's shit here,' she mumbled to herself. 'Total fucking shit.' She looked at the fountain, at the big, bearded bastard, probably God, standing on top where he was flanked by a pair of big stone tarts, and at the poxy jets of water shooting out from stupid angles. It was like something from the outside part of Homebase, only bigger and more fake-looking. The place was heaving with tourists. Lots of them were couples who were so in love that they didn't even notice the rain. Others, mainly teenagers, huddled together in groups and threw their money into the water. She couldn't work out why there were so many people there looking at something which was, if you thought about it sensibly for a moment, complete rubbish. People were taking photographs of a man wrestling a horse, and some were so delirious just to be there that they stood precariously on the fountain's edge and were whistled down by policemen. There was a shop on one side of the piazza selling shoes and bags, and a shop on the other side of the piazza selling bags and shoes. She wondered what kind of fucking idiot would buy bags or shoes from either of those shops. 'What a complete load of utter fucking shit,' she said.

She took a bar of horrible Italian chocolate from her bag. As she unwrapped it, a dog came up to her and sat down. He looked up at her expectantly.

'No,' she said.

She saw a hungry look in his eyes.

'No,' she said, snapping off and eating a square of the chocolate. The dog hadn't responded to either English or Italian, so she tried Welsh. 'Na, chei di ddim.'

The dog shuffled closer. She looked at him, and he cocked his head to one side. 'All right then. One piece.' She threw it high, and the dog leapt up and caught it. She wasn't enjoying the chocolate at all, but knew of its importance in times of trouble. She had read that eating chocolate was supposed to be like having sex. It was something to do with chemicals. She thought about that for a while.

Eating chocolate was probably better than having sex with her old boyfriend, but it didn't come close to being as good as having sex with Enrico. Having sex with Enrico in Tenby had been the best thing she had ever done. She broke off and ate another square. It seemed to do her a bit of good. Having never been really heartbroken before, she was surprised by the violence of her feelings. It was as though a ferret were desperately trying to escape from her body. She had always thought that when people sang songs of pain, they were singing only about emotional pain, but this pain was physical too, and her body was hurting like never before. She felt it behind her eyeballs and it reminded her of what strange things eyes were, which was something she hadn't thought about since she had been about six. She felt it in her teeth and across her shoulders and, most unexpectedly of all, she felt it in her shins. They felt as though they were about to shatter, that if she stood up they would crumble. That must be the pain in the songs. It was the hurting deep inside. 'How are your shins?' she asked the dog. 'Are they OK?'

The dog watched her fingers as they snapped off more chocolate, and caught his second piece.

'I wish I was you,' she said. A man walked past selling roses. Guided by instinct, he left her alone. She and the dog took turns eating the chocolate until it was all gone. She thought of how sad her boyfriend back home must have been when she had called him from Tenby to tell him she had been doing some thinking. She understood why he had cried, and why he had written her long letters telling her she was a fucking bitch. In one of his letters he had told her every detail of his dream for the future. She was there, and so were two boys and two girls, a Labrador called Jumbo Jet and a little house near the sea. It was pathetic. She shivered, and wanted to tell him she was sorry. She stroked the dog's head. 'Oes angen bwyd arnat ti o hyd? Oes e? I'm starving. Let's find something else to eat,' she said. She ached as she stood up.

She found a place selling filled rolls, and bought two. One for her, and one for the dog. 'Here you go,' she said, throwing his onto the ground. He left most of the salad, but seemed to enjoy the rest of it. When she had finished hers she went back inside and bought two more, one without salad. She knew enough Italian for that.

'I,' she said to the dog, as he ate his second roll, 'am your best friend.' She stroked his head. 'You can't get enough of me. You love me.'

She walked on, down a dark street, and he followed as she knew he would. 'Have you got rabies?' she asked him. 'Have you? Do you want to bite me? Is that what this is all about? Are you just waiting for the right moment to pounce? Do it now.' She stopped, and held out her arm to him. 'Bite me.' He sniffed it, and she smiled. 'So much for rabies,' she said.

'I'm soaked.' She hadn't really thought about it until then. 'You wouldn't understand. You don't mind the wet. You're a dog.'

She also noticed that the ache coming from the knuckles on her right hand wasn't caused by the pain of separation, but from the punch that had landed on Enrico's cheek. She had never hit anyone before, but had been coached enough times by her brother. He would hold a cushion, tell her it was Amanda Jones's face, and get her to hit it. 'Harder,' he would say, every time. 'Imagine it's six inches further back than it really is, and aim there. That way your fist keeps up its momentum. It's like not slowing down until you've crossed the finishing line.' He had taught her how to put her weight into it, and told her the best parts of the face to aim for. He always told her he knew lots of different fighting techniques, but that she would only need so many as a girl. He was confident he had taught his sister how to do damage if the need arose. She had never quite got round to hitting Amanda Jones, but her training came back in a flash when it came to hitting Enrico. It had been a hard punch. Her brother would have been proud of her. He might not have been quite so proud of her walking around the Palatine Hill with no underwear on, or the way she and her Roman had fucked almost silently in the toilet of a Chinese restaurant, but he would have been proud of her for hitting the bastard so hard it hurt. She would tell him about it when she got home. Beaten up by a girl.

The dog showed no sign of going away. 'You *really* love me, don't you? And because I'm a nice person I'm not going to send you away. I'm going to love you back. And to prove that I love you I'm going to give you even more food.' She bought what she thought must be chestnuts from a man on a corner, and when they had cooled down they shared them. She sat on a bench and the dog sat in front of her, looking up. He didn't seem too keen, but he ate them anyway. 'I don't have to stay slim now. Not now nobody loves me. Except you, that is. You love me.'

She fiddled with his ears. 'What's your name?' she asked. The dog looked up at her, and wagged his tail. 'I could call you Teg,' she said. 'Or maybe I'll call you Huw.' She missed her friend Huw. She told him everything. She had told him about Enrico before she had even told her boyfriend about him. In fact she had never told her boyfriend about Enrico. What she had told him was that there was nobody else, but that she felt their lives were going in different directions. Sitting on the bench with the dog's ears in between her fingers, she decided that her friend Huw was her favourite person, the first one she would call when she got home. She thought about all the afternoons they had spent in his room watching videos, drinking cider until they could only just stand up, talking about anything, and laughing until they could hardly breathe. He had never tried to kiss her, not even when they were really drunk, which she thought was strange. She occasionally gave him a big *you've-got-to-follow-your-heart* speech, and told him there was nothing to be ashamed of and that he should go to Bristol or somewhere else he could get a boyfriend. He would hit her with a pillow. She had sent him a postcard of the Vittorio Emanuele Monument, telling him she thought he would like to see it himself one day, that it was easily the most openly homosexual building she had ever seen. She had put it in an envelope so his mum and dad wouldn't read it. She realised she hadn't thought of Enrico for a few minutes.

'I'm out of love,' she said, kissing the top of the dog's head. 'I'm out of love, and it's all thanks to you.' But then her shins started to hurt again, and she thought of Enrico, and the way he would hold her, and she cried.

She decided to call him Teg after all. She didn't know why, not that it mattered one way or the other. She found a stall and bought a lot more chocolate and a bottle of champagne. She didn't really want to drink champagne, but she wanted some booze and she didn't have a corkscrew, and anyway it was too cheap to be real champagne so it wouldn't seem like celebrating. She sat on a low wall, watching people going into nightclubs, and fired the cork down the pavement. Teg ran after it and brought it back, which was very impressive. He was rewarded with a big piece of chocolate. At one point he crouched down and was about to shit on the pavement, but she pushed him over to the roadside just in time. Her clothes had dried out a bit, but not completely. The sky had cleared, and the night had grown cold. She was uncomfortable, and started thinking about when she should go back to her hotel. Her flight was at half past eleven in the morning, so she guessed somewhere around seven. She would stay out until then, shivering. She wondered what she would do if Enrico was there. She pictured him waiting for her on Via Firenze, frantic with worry, then telling her he had broken it off with that other girl, that he loved her more than words could say, and that nothing was more important to him than being with her. She wondered whether she would take him back. She just didn't know. She had no idea. Yes she did. She would take him back like a shot.

She was worried about what all the chocolate might be doing to Teg's insides. She wondered where she could get dog biscuits in Rome at two o'clock in the morning. 'Come on,' she said. 'You need a balanced diet.' They walked on. She held the scruff of his neck as they crossed the road, even though he automatically walked to heel and there weren't too many cars around to run him over.

She couldn't find a place selling dog biscuits, but she thought that the plain Pringles and popcorn she found on a stall would have a similar effect. 'Everyone likes Pringles,' she said, as she emptied half a long tube on to the pavement.

She walked on, sometimes throwing Teg a piece of popcorn, which he would leap up to catch. She thought about taking up smoking. She had thought about that quite a lot since being in Rome, not because she wanted to smoke, but because she wanted to hold a cigarette at that particular angle, like Italian girls. Now she wanted to smoke because dying young no longer seemed like such a bad idea.

They happened to walk past the Pantheon. She had been inside it twice, once when it was sunny and she could see the clouds through the hole in the roof, and then again when there was a shower. She had pictured herself there with a couple of excited children, a girl and a boy, holding out their tiny half-Italian hands to catch the raindrops. But Enrico had killed their babies. He might as well have dropped rocks on their beautiful soft heads. Looking at it again the building reminded her of a gas works. Nobody was around. The sound of a plastic bag being blown along the ground made her jump, but it didn't really frighten her because she had Teg there with her.

*　　*　　*

Just before seven they started walking back to the hotel. She thought about what she would do when she got back to Wales. She knew her mum would wrap her up in blankets and feed her soup, as if she had a cold, and that when her mum was out of the room her dad would give her shots of brandy and tell her to down them in one. Then she would go back to work, and start getting ready to go away to college. And when she got to college she would put a photo of Teg on her pin board, and people would point at it and say, 'Is that your dog?' and she would tell them that he wasn't. She would tell them about her trip to Rome, and how horrible it had been, and all about how she had spent her last night with a dog who had followed her everywhere. She would tell them how she wished she could have brought him home, but had known all along that she wouldn't be able to, not without money.

She reached Via Delle Quattro Fontane, and knew which roads would get her back to the hotel. She couldn't believe she had liked the four fountains so much when she had first seen them.

Four ugly people lying down was not such a big deal. She had spent a summer in Tenby. She had seen hundreds of ugly people lying down.

She reached the hotel, and crouched down outside. 'Listen,' she said. 'You stay out here, and I'll go and get my camera. I'll be back in two minutes, so don't go away.' She poured the last of the popcorn on to the pavement, raced to her room, and took her camera from the bedside table. It struck her that it would be full of pictures of Enrico, and that when she got it back from the chemist she would have to get her brother to take out all the pictures of him and throw them in the bin, and only leave the photos of the dog. She had four pictures left out of thirty-six.

She ran downstairs and went outside. The popcorn was gone, and so was Teg. She ran along the street calling his name, but just kept making a nuisance of herself by nearly bumping into people. She reached Via Nazionale, and looked both ways. He wasn't there. She knew she wasn't going to find him, so she walked back to the hotel where she would get them to call a taxi for her, and wait for it to come along and take her to the airport.

In the lobby she took her camera out of its pouch and flipped open the back. She pulled the film out of its cartridge, exposing it to the yellow light. She put it in an ashtray. It spilled over the sides. She hoped Teg would be OK.

He was a few streets away, heading south at about four miles an hour.

Cockroft woke up, his dehydrated brain just slightly too small for his skull. He was still in his clothes, and he could smell himself. He staggered to his feet and went down into the kitchen, where he poured himself a pint of water. He drank it in one, then poured himself another. He looked over to Timoleon Vieta's chair, and remembered what they had done the night before.

'He'll be fine,' he said to himself, his pink eyes fixed on the flattened, hair-covered cushions. 'You'll be fine, Timoleon Vieta. Don't you worry.'

He took his glass back to his room, and fell asleep with his shoes still on.

SOMETHING CHINESE

The dog walked quickly along the streets, his belly low, staying close to walls, dashing across busy roads, and sometimes stopping to eat something that had been dropped. His tail hung still behind him.

Mai's father, May's husband, loved his wife and daughter so much that he couldn't stop thinking about them. He always took a laminated photograph of them to work, and whenever he found a quiet moment he would take it out of his wallet and look at it, at his wife looking down at the baby in her arms, and at the toothless baby smiling up at him as he held the camera. He loved them so much that his every moment was blighted by the feeling that he wasn't doing enough for them. Even though he had risen to become a foreman for a big construction set up, and was starting to earn reasonable money, he could never escape the feeling that his wife deserved better clothes and a few more modern appliances for their small apartment, and that his daughter should have had bigger and brighter toys to play with. So as he sat at the card table it was always with a vision of the future in his mind – May in a thick winter coat, and Mai on a colourful plastic tricycle, her little legs whirling like wind turbines as she charged up and down the street where they lived. He played well and kept on winning, and before long he had enough money to start laying large stakes. He took his gambling away from his circle of friends, to people who were more serious about it and who played for a bit more money. As his debts reached the point where the only hope he had of ever repaying them was to keep playing until he hit another winning streak, it was with his wife and child in his mind's eye that he returned to the table time and time again. They were there before him, shining like angels as he was tied up, gagged and beaten to death with a baseball bat halfway down a quiet street in a small town not far from the city.

It was the professor's fourth time in Shanghai. His duties were fairly light. For four months, while a Chinese academic sat in classes in Italy talking about Chinese culture and history, he gave lectures at one of the universities and sat in classes answering questions about various aspects of European culture and history, particularly the Roman Empire and the Second World War. The exchange didn't make him any extra money, but he was always very well looked after, and when the invitation came around every two or three years he accepted it straight away. He had nobody to stay in Italy for, and he could never resist the lure of the university's library. He was timetabled for just two or three hours a day, and spent most of his spare time exploring the bookshelves – preparing lectures, studying ancient and modern Chinese dialects and looking for anything to do with the country's history that might be of interest to his students or colleagues back in Rome. He always returned home with enough material for a paper on something, and he had earned a solid reputation in the field.

Late on his second Tuesday morning, his duties over for the day, he went looking for an old book on the Age of Division that he had been referring to the day before. It wasn't there. Looking to see whether it had been shuffled out of place, he noticed someone by his side. It was a small woman of about thirty, with short hair.

'Were you looking for this?' she whispered, holding the book out to him.

'Yes, but I can read something else until you've finished with it.' He had grown quite used to the local dialect, and could speak it very well. Whenever he was in the country he took lessons to make sure he hadn't fallen into bad habits. He talked with his colleagues in their language, and to keep in touch with the way the language was spoken by people in everyday situations he made a point of talking about food with people in cheap restaurants, and about the weather with old men in the park. These conversations almost always developed in interesting directions, and he hardly ever needed the interpreter who stood alongside him as he taught.

'No, please, take it.' She looked nervous. 'I shouldn't be here anyway. I'm sorry.'

'So you don't work here?' She didn't look like a student, and he had assumed she was a librarian.

'Yes, I work here, but I'm not a librarian. I'm a cleaner. I come to the university very early in the morning and I'm supposed to go home when I finish my shift. They turn a blind eye to me coming here and reading for an hour or two each day, but if I start taking books away from the lecturers or the students I could get in trouble, so please . . .' Again she held the book out to him. 'Anyway, I should go home now.'

He wanted to carry on whispering to her about the book that they clearly shared an interest in, but someone else had come into their aisle to browse. He took the book from her, and put it in its place on the shelf. 'Let me see you to the door,' he said.

He persuaded her to join him for a cup of tea at a shop just down the street from the library. Passing students cast curious glances at the sight of the white-haired European professor engrossed in conversation with someone they weren't sure they recognised but who might have been a cleaner at the university. They were talking so intently about things that may or may not have happened centuries ago that they didn't notice anybody looking in their direction. The old man was surprised, and a little embarrassed, to find that she knew more about the period between the Han and Sui dynasties than he did. Like him she knew exactly who controlled which parts of China at which point in time, but she could also recite pages of poetry by Cao Cao, Cao Pei and Cao Zhi, and point to political allusions between the lines. After a while the woman excused herself, saying she had people waiting for her at home.

Two days later they met again, not far from the same shelf in the library, and they continued their conversation over tea at the same table as before. After about half an hour they stopped talking about the distant past. She told him about her three-year-old daughter, and all about how her husband had disappeared almost a year before, and how his body had never been found. She told the professor that she didn't nurse any romantic notions of him dramatically coming back into her life. She knew, and everybody knew, that he was dead. She had loved him, she said, and she missed him, but she had always known he had been half stupid. He had tried hard to hide his gambling from her, just as his friends tried to hide their gambling from their wives, but she had known about it all along. All she hadn't known about until it was too late was the extent of the trouble he had been in. She had thought he had still been playing cards with his friends for a bit of beer money, but when he went missing they told her that they hadn't played with him for months, that he played with a group of people they didn't know. She supposed he had died like somebody in a bad film from Hong Kong, killed as an example by the people he owed money to, in front of a petrified audience of debtors who had a more realistic chance of meeting their payments. She was grateful that whoever it was who had killed him had left her and her little girl alone. They must have known that they had nothing worth taking. She told the old man all about how she and the girl had moved in with her cousin's family, where they shared a small room in an eight storey flat with four other people, and that even though she brought a small amount of money into the house from her job, she was feeling more and more like an intruder as other children in the house grew up and took up more space. She said she was hoping for more hours at the university, so she could maybe begin to live a little more independently. She dreaded having to find work elsewhere and move away from the books. She told him she had always wanted to go to university but had never been able to afford it, and anyway she had married young. Her job was, she said, the next best thing. She told him that she looked forward to one day passing on everything she had learned to her little girl. Every day she read books for as long as she could, always feeling guilty because the people who watched Mai thought that she always rushed home the moment she finished her shift. Sometimes she chose a book at random, and sometimes she found a seam that interested her and pursued it for weeks at a time. For a while she had done nothing but study the English language. She was pleased with her progress and had little difficulty learning to read and write, but without anyone to practise with she had no idea how the words sounded, so she had given up. She said that maybe she should start learning Italian.

The old man felt almost like a child as he told her all about his life in Italy – all those years spent shut away in libraries, lecturing and occasionally publishing academic papers and specialist books. Really, there was nothing much to tell.

'I think it's strange that you never married,' she said.

'Yes,' he said. 'I suppose it is strange.'

But it wasn't long before the conversation took them back to the past. He wasn't surprised that he knew more about some aspects of the recent history of China than she did, having had access to materials that weren't readily available inside the country and having followed developments there closely for as long as he could remember. They only ever talked about this in low voices, even when there was nobody else around. He found talking to her a lot more satisfying than talking to other academics, whose ideas were set in stone, and who had published works and reputations to defend, and who clung to their opinions as though they were the last drop of water in the desert. He knew that he too had been guilty of this at times. May thought nothing of shooting off on wild tangents, which always seemed to make some kind of sense in the end, or changing her viewpoint on any subject they happened to be talking about, sometimes even halfway through a sentence.

They started meeting at museums and galleries. After a while May started to take her little girl along with her. At first Mai found the old man frightening, and hid behind her mother whenever he was around, but after they had met a few times she decided that she liked him. The old man would pick her up and dangle her over cabinets so she could get a clearer view of the exhibits. She found this wildly entertaining, her giggles resounding around the cavernous rooms.

After a visit to an exhibition of nineteenth-century ceramics they arranged, almost without thinking, for their next meeting to be not at the library or a place of great cultural significance, but at Hongkou Park, where Mai would be able to run around and make as much noise as she liked, and where they could treat her to whichever sweet things were for sale and take her boating on the lake.

A few days later, while they were eating noodles in a run-down cafe, they started laughing at themselves – the old man from a distant land and the young widow. When they had finished laughing they felt like teenagers in the moments before their first kiss, neither of them knowing what to do or say.

*   *   *

Having expected a cold, manipulative beauty queen, the professor's relatives were surprised by his wife's friendly manner, her unremarkable looks, her ordinary clothes and her hair that was cut almost like a man's. They found themselves unexpectedly impressed by her solid grasp of basic Italian. Her four-year-old daughter was quiet, and seemed pleasant enough as she played on her own. They still couldn't quite understand what the old man was doing getting married for the first time at his age, but as they could find nothing to dislike about his wife or his step daughter they gave up worrying about him. 'I suppose we should just leave him to it,' they said to one another on the telephone.

The professor carried on working, leaving his wife to cook, shop, play with her daughter, study Italian and plough through all the Chinese books on his shelves. On weekends they did family things like visiting ruins and museums, having picnics in the park and driving to the coast. The old man was fond of Mai. He enjoyed watching her playing quietly, but found it difficult to talk to her. He read stories to her at bedtime, with her mother there to help him along, but when it came to everyday conversation he was stuck. He didn't know what small children liked to talk about, and when she told him things he already knew he had difficulty feigning interest, unable to understand why she thought he needed to be told that she was building a tower of plastic bricks or wearing a red T-shirt when it was so very obvious. He let his wife attend to the mechanics of having a child around the place. She was always the one who fed her when she was hungry, and wiped her nose and her chin. The old man couldn't stand to see the little girl eat. The spillages around her mouth looked like vomit and put him off his own food, and during meals he concentrated very hard on not looking at her messy face. Whenever Mai threw a tantrum he would leave the room, letting her mother discipline her, which she always did in Italian. They rarely talked freely in Chinese until after the child had gone to bed. Then they worked together on pieces for various academic journals, starting with a paper on the political allusions to be found in the poetry of Cao Cao, Cao Pei and Cao Zhi. When May was at her language classes Maria, a woman from across the street whose own children had left home, came to their house to mind Mai, and always told the professor what a delight she had been to look after – how well behaved, happy and gentle.

May settled into her new life very quickly. Her Italian improved every day, she gradually got the hang of the cuisine, and when she met the other mothers in the neighbourhood she was so complimentary of their children that it wasn't long before people were saying it seemed as though she had lived in Italy all her life. People who knew her were genuinely upset when one day, as she was on her way to her language class, a van's back tyre burst and the driver lost control and mounted the pavement, slamming her into a wall.

The old man never went back to work. Finding himself, at sixty-eight, the only parent of a six-year-old girl, he didn't know what to do. He arranged for Maria to come in early in the morning to get her up and get her ready for school, and again in the evening to cook for both of them and to give the little girl her bath and put her to bed. He frantically read books about parenting, trying as hard as he could to make sense of all the conflicting advice. He never stopped worrying about her.

When she started school he walked her to the gate every morning and waved goodbye. As soon as he got home he started preparing for her return – learning the rules to childish board games and devising ways of keeping her busy and infusing her with an enthusiasm for the world around her.

Mai always looked forward to the end of school. All day she wanted to go home to where she would hear about things that were much more interesting than anything she had learned at school, and where nobody was going to flick rolled up bits of paper at the back of her head, or tip her satchel upside down and laugh at her as she scrabbled around for her pens and pencils, or tell her that she had a flat face. She took to her lessons at home with such enthusiasm that she hardly ever asked to play games. The old man taught her about the natural world, about different countries and about things that had happened a long time ago. He made up funny stories about anything he happened to be teaching her. She never stopped being amazed by the way he seemed to know everything – she never asked a question to which she did not receive an interesting answer. As she grew older she became increasingly disappointed with her teachers at school when they couldn't answer questions about exactly how many heads Hydra had by the time it was finally killed by Heracles, about the weather in the days preceding the Seige of Lisbon, or the differences between the Mercalli and Richter scales.

Encouraged by the old man, she always drew and painted. No matter what he was teaching her about, at some point she would sit at the kitchen table with her coloured pencils, crayons or paints and create her own picture of it. The old man loved every one of them, knowing exactly what each picture was supposed to be. Soon the walls of the house were covered with Colorado beetles in acrylic, Mata Hari in wax crayon, Christians clamped between the jaws of lions, Rossini at work on *The Barber Of Seville*, El Lute, an iron lung, the war graves of Belgium and dozens of other subjects. With each new picture the old man became increasingly convinced that she was a natural artist.

On visits to relatives Mai was given instructions to present them with an original piece of art. As soon as the door opened the professor looked proudly on as she thrust into the hands of this sister or that cousin a cross-section of a Viking long ship, a map of the Basque country, a picture of a Cro-Magnon herder crouching over his fire, or a depiction of Angkor Thom in the time of Indravarman III, complete with naked women bathing and men having their gall bladders forcibly removed.

Before his marriage his social calls had been rare, and had followed a simple pattern – he made a few polite inquiries, paid no attention to the answers he was given, ate whatever was on offer, muttered incomprehensibly about whichever piece of research he was engrossed in at the time, then sat and stared into the middle distance for a while before suddenly remembering a pressing engagement and promising an imminent return visit which everybody knew wouldn't really happen for months, and sometimes even years. Concerned for Mai to feel as though she were a part of a large family who loved her, he became a social butterfly, visiting people at least once a week. He wouldn't stop talking about what she had done at school, what he had taught her at home and, when she was out of earshot, how extraordinarily intelligent and talented she was.

He had thought so much about her future that it seemed as real to him as their day to day lives. Most of these thoughts he kept to himself. He didn't want her to feel as though she was under too much pressure, and anyway he was sure she would get there under her own steam. He had decided that Mai was going to get better and better at painting, and when she had finished school she would continue taking art classes as she studied meteorology or zoology or whichever subject she chose to pursue at university. Outshining her contemporaries at everything she put her hand to, she would find a job she loved and, on the side, begin to exhibit and sell her paintings. Maybe he would even help her run her own gallery. In the midst of all this she would marry – not to an academic, as he couldn't think of a single one he had ever encountered who would be good enough for her, but probably to a successful and highly regarded young doctor. Her husband would be so wild with love for her that he would never let her down, and after a year of marriage she would have a baby. He wouldn't mind if it was a boy or a girl. Not long after cradling the child in his arms, kissing its forehead and its big, fat cheeks, he would fall asleep in his chair in the back garden and never wake up. It would be a warm evening in April. He had worked it out. He would be eighty-seven.

A week before Mai's thirteenth birthday the old man had already bought her several presents and hidden them in his room. There was a life-size plastic skeleton, an easel and a box of paints, some sheet music for the piano she was learning to play, and a pile of books.

'What would you like to do on your birthday?' he asked over breakfast.

'Nothing.'

'But we always do something. You could invite your friends here – I could get Maria to arrange a party. You would enjoy it.'

'I told you. I don't want a party.'

'Well, then we should go somewhere then. Where would you like to go?'

Mai shook her head. 'I don't want to go anywhere. I don't want to do anything. Just forget about it,' she snapped. 'Leave me alone.'

The old man had never seen her like this before. His breathing quickened, and he could feel his heart pounding in the silence. He felt he had to say something. 'What's wrong, Mai?'

She told him what was wrong. She told him that he was not her real father, and he would never be her real father; that if it hadn't been for him her mother, who she could hardly even remember, would still be alive; that she would never really be Italian; that she wasn't Chinese any more; that everything she had ever heard him say had been boring; that she had always hated drawing pictures; that she didn't have any friends;

that she hated him, and that she wished she had never been born. She picked up her bag and went to school.

The slamming of the door seemed distant and muffled, as though it were a sound effect in a radio soap. The old man struggled for breath. He stood up, holding on to the table for support. Everything around him swam as he made his way to the front door, and his ears began to scream. He wanted to run after her, to catch up with her and tell her how sorry he was that he had wasted her time with his stupid lessons and stories, that he had taken her away from China, that he had tried so hard to be a father to her and that he had made such a terrible mess of her life.

His legs felt like lead as he stumbled into the street. 'I'm sorry Mai,' he said, trying to shout in case she was still within earshot, but his voice was just a dry whisper. He looked for her, but she had gone. As he made his way towards her school the houses on either side of the street grew darker and darker until they were black, ugly blocks that closed in on him, surrounding him until he could see nothing, and all he could feel was a pain in his chest, as though someone were stabbing him and twisting the blade.

It was mid-morning when Maria arrived at Mai's school. In the small room where they were sent when they thought they were about to throw up, Mai heard all about how he had been found lying in the street, and how the doctors had done their best to save him but that they couldn't, no matter how hard they tried.

'It happens to a lot of old people,' she said, her arms wrapped tightly around the trembling girl. 'Sometimes their hearts just stop, and there's nothing in the world that will make them start beating again.'

Mai was the only child at the funeral, and was the only person crying as the old man's coffin was lowered into the ground. All the other people there, all his relatives and former colleagues, were dry-eyed and expressionless. She told herself she was the only one there who had really known him, and loved him, which made it all the more unbearable for her to think that it was all her fault, that if it wasn't for her, if she hadn't been so horrible to him, he would still be alive.

She wiped her tears, and through a gap in the adults she saw a dog skulking along the perimeter of the cemetery, sixty or seventy metres away. Even from such a distance she noticed how sad it looked, and how lovely, and she ached to go up and run her hands along its fur and to tickle behind its ears. She thought that maybe if she made friends with it and they couldn't find its owner she would be allowed to keep it. She wondered whose job it was to decide whether or not she was allowed to do things like that. She would call it something Chinese. Slowly and quietly she broke away from the other mourners. When she was a little way away from them she sped towards the dog. Nobody noticed she had gone until she tripped over the corner of a grave and they heard a thud and a sharp cry as she landed awkwardly on the ground. One of the women went to see if she was all right, while everyone else silently wondered what was going to happen to the strange little girl that the old man had brought back from China, who hardly ever said anything and who had drawn all those awful pictures.

Startled by the commotion, the dog ran back in the direction he had come from. He moved with a sense of confidence, as if he had been lost and had suddenly found himself on the right track. His tail in the air, he left the graveyard and crossed the road. He was heading, roughly, north.

In 1974 Cockroft had written the theme tune and incidental music for a television comedy series called *Turk Is A Four-Letter Word*. The programme followed the progress of a Turkish immigrant who, along with his wife and children, had moved into a quiet suburban cul-de-sac. Every week the plot revolved around the Turk trying to help a neighbour or tackle a burglar or assist the community in some other way, but his intentions were always comically misinterpreted. He would end each episode alone, often in police custody, wondering aloud what he could do to prove to society that he was well-meaning and neighbourly.

The programme was hugely popular, and the Turk's catch phrase, *But I was only trying to help*, swept the nation, but it attracted accusations of racism and irresponsibility in a turbulent political climate. Cockroft, by then a well-known bandleader and bon-viveur, the producer and the programme's star were invited on to a BBC2 discussion programme to face their detractors. It was broadcast live, and started very well. The star of the show, himself the son of Turkish immigrants, began by saying that of course a large proportion of the comedy of their show was drawn from racist attitudes but that they were mocking and effectively belittling these attitudes, not endorsing them. The producer spoke for a while about his sense of social responsibility, and then came Cockroft's turn. He had only been invited at the last minute because the show's writer had been suffering from a grumbling appendix, but he was a regular on radio panel shows and quite used to live broadcasting so he spoke with assurance and confidence. He started by acknowledging that of course the show was racist, but that it was affectionately racist. Pressed to explain exactly what he meant by *affectionately racist*, Cockroft, who had relaxed backstage by drinking three-quarters of a bottle of brandy, explained.

He explained that of course Britain was, for better or for worse, in a way, a sort of multi-cultural society, and that he welcomed the contributions of a number of the people who had come to Britain from other parts of the world – particularly their restaurants and their lovely carnivals. Nudged by the presenter, he explained that he believed the immigrants who were already in the country should be able to stay if they really wanted to, but only if they were prepared to assimilate fully into British society. He continued by declaring that the reality was that they did all live in a racist nation, and that Enoch Powell was right, enough was enough. If many more foreigners were to come into the country there would indeed be rivers of blood. Turk would turn against Greek, the Jew against the Egyptian, and Nigerians would fight the Irish in the streets. His face had turned purple and his fists were clenched by the time he concluded by proclaiming great friendship with a number of shopkeepers and restaurateurs from Bangladesh, Uganda and even Turkey. 'I've got nothing against foreigners whatsoever,' he bellowed. 'But for their sake and for ours we have to take a practical approach and say *enough is enough*. England,' he said, 'must remain English, and that means pulling up the drawbridge and, frankly, encouraging as many of them as we can to go back to where they came from.'

Thanking everyone for their contributions, the presenter moved on to the next part of the programme. The second series of *Turk Is A Four-Letter Word*, which was already at an advanced stage of production, was cancelled, as was its spin-off series, *It's All Greek To Me*. Cockroft never worked again.

'It was awful,' he said to the Bosnian, who was staring into the distance. 'All my work went to other people. People who weren't racists like me.

I tried to explain, but nobody would listen. I tried to apologise. I called the newspapers, but they just weren't interested in doing anything other than burying me alive or making me look stupid in cartoons. I wanted to tell them I hadn't meant it, but I could hardly say I had been cruelly abandoned that morning by a Moroccan businessman, and that I was having some kind of personal crisis. I was only a racist for a day. Everyone's a racist for a day at some point in their lives.' His voice cracked. 'I didn't mean those things I said. In fact I've always been rather liberal.' He stubbed out his cigar on the ground. 'I say, *Love your brother*.' He looked at the Bosnian, who was still staring into the distance. 'I was drunk, for God's sake. Doesn't everyone say things they don't mean when they're drunk?' The Bosnian carried on staring at nothing in particular. 'Don't go telling me you've never done anything you've regretted when you've been drunk.' He took another swig of wine. 'Don't give me that crap.' Cockroft was slurring.

'And do you know what the worst thing was? The day after the programme I went to a fancy dress party. I hadn't heard anything about all the fuss. I hadn't read the papers, and nobody had called me to tell me I was public enemy number one. I went as Henry the Eighth. Henry the fucking Eighth. Can you believe that? So I turn up, fashionably late, bound into the room and shout, *Off with her head*. And what happens? The music stops. Someone's pulled the plug on the stereo. Then the lights come up and everyone starts shouting things. *Fuck off Cockroft. Off with your own head, you wanker*. Then someone throws a glass of wine over me. Sweet white wine. Liebfraumilch. Some fucking Liebfraumilch drinker thinks they have the right to come over all superior. And I get pushed out into the street. There are no cabs, so I get the bus. Dressed as Henry the Eighth, crying my eyes out and stinking out the top deck with sweet white wine.' The combination of alcohol and anger had, as often happened, reawoken the Westcountry accent of his childhood. He started drinking from the bottle. 'Henry the fucking Eighth. And who stood by me? Who stood up and said *Cockroft's not so bad, let's give him another chance*? Not one single fucker. Not a one. Everyone in the business decided they'd never liked me in the first place. Suddenly they forgot all the times they'd come to parties at my flat, they forgot about how I let them fuck their foul-mouthed rent boys in my spare room and never told a soul. All I got was a handful of letters, mainly from branches of the National Front inviting me to speak at their rallies. Nobody from the business even tried to get in touch with a gesture of friendship. I had an enthusiastic note of support from someone called Eric Clapton, telling me he agreed with everything I'd said on television, that he also thought Britain was overcrowded. There was something that looked like a lump of sick on the paper. I've still got no idea if it was the real Eric Clapton, but just in case it was I sent a note to his record company telling him he could take his slow hand and shove it up his arse. I wasn't a real racist, I had just been having a bad day.'

The Bosnian was still just staring into the distance, as if the old man wasn't there at all.

'So that was that,' said Cockroft, calming down.

'It was all over. One minute I was on top of the world, and the next I'd had it. Finished. All because I'd gone on a poxy discussion show that nobody was watching anyway.' He had relived these memories time and time again.

'There I was, in all my glory. Cockroft, the housewives' favourite, railing in a kipper tie against the Mohammedans.'

The thick, still heat had been oppressive all day, and Cockroft was on his fourth shirt. Clouds moved in and it started to rain, so they went inside.

GIUSEPPE, OR LEONARDO DA VINCI

Timoleon Vieta killed and ate rats and rabbits and old, slow hares. He scavenged from bins outside houses, turning them over in the middle of the night and eating as much as he could before being chased away by angry people. When he wasn't rattling bins he was almost like a ghost, slinking along barely noticed, his skinny belly close to the ground. But he carried on heading home. Tired, hungry and alone.

Aurora was sitting at one end of the bench, two hundred and twenty pages into a book about spinal injuries that she had found in the local library.

It had been published nineteen years earlier, two years before she was born. She knew a lot of it to be out of date, but it held her attention and she made occasional notes in a pad. She was hoping to go to medical school.

Sitting at the other end of the bench was a boy she recognised. She had spent many hours with her grandmother discussing the terrible things he was said to have done. The old lady had told her that he had been in trouble for small things, but that everybody knew him to be involved in much more than those forgivable juvenile crimes for which he had been caught red-handed. She had heard reports of stolen motor bikes, fights, vandalism and all kinds of unsavoury misdemeanours that she was loath to tell her granddaughter about, but told her just the same. He was, she would say, a slippery one – he seemed to be able to make himself invisible for as long as it took to get away with causing trouble. Aurora had been instructed to stay away from him.

He was watching a house across the street. Having heard that the family who lived there was due to attend a funeral in Montevardi the following day, he was waiting for them to leave so he could break in through their kitchen window and take whatever he could find. He wasn't expecting much, probably just a video recorder, some CDs and a bit of jewellery, but he was sure it would just about be worth his while. He had a feel for these things. They seemed to be taking forever to pack their cars. At least three generations were charging backwards and forwards.

He noticed the girl waving a piece of paper in his direction.

He took it. On it she had written, *What's the time?* He showed her his watch, and went back to looking at the family of mourners interminably packing their two cars. He had heard that the funeral was to be for a nine-year-old girl who had died of some kind of blood disease.

He sensed another piece of paper being held in his direction. Irritated by the distraction, and wishing the girl would go away, he snatched it from her hand. It read, *Thank you.* He stuffed it into his shirt pocket.

Having filled the car with boxes and bags, instead of simply driving away to Montevardi and the body of the little girl, the family went back into the house and shut the door. With nothing left to watch the boy became restless. He took the *Thank you* note out of his pocket, turned it over on to its blank side, and took the girl's pen from her hand.

He wrote, *YOU ARE DEAF*, and gave the piece of paper back to her. He remembered an afternoon three or four years before, when he and some friends had walked behind her for a while, shouting dirty words that they had known she couldn't hear.

She read the note, and underneath wrote, *I know*. She handed it back.

He took her pad, turned to a blank page at the back, and wrote, *DO YOU GO TO DEAF SCHOOL?*

She moved closer to watch him as he slowly formed the capital letters. He felt her breath on his neck. When he had finished she took the pen and paper. *Yes*, she wrote. *Deaf and blind school. They put us together because they thought we would get along.*

DO YOU LIKE BLIND PEOPLE?
In general, yes. They're OK.

They talked about her school, about his bad behaviour, about this and that. For the first time in ages he found himself enjoying a conversation. He even used words he had never written down before. She crossed out his obscenities, and ignored his spelling mistakes. Aurora became later and later for her evening meal, and the cars left for Montevardi unnoticed, but the new friends could not stop talking.

Within five pages they had exchanged solemn vows of love. Arranging to meet the following day, they went their separate ways.

Later, as he drifted through the streets in a daze, he met the man with whom he had arranged to pass on his pickings from the empty house. He hadn't been expecting to make a great deal of money, but had known he would get a fair price for whatever it was he had taken. He and the older man had known each other for a while, and trusted each other.

'So?' asked the man.

'What?'

'So did you get into that house?'

'Oh, that.' He hadn't spared the empty house a thought. 'No, I didn't.'

'Why not?'

'Oh, you know.' He sighed, and looked up at the stars. 'I just don't do that kind of thing any more.' He walked away.

They met every day. As she got off the bus after school he would be waiting for her, usually leaning against a wall a short distance away from the bus stop. As soon as they had found a flat surface to rest on, they talked about everything that came into their minds. No topic was too grand or too trivial. Sometimes they wrote at once on different parts of the same page. If he finished before her, which he often did, he drew pictures that made her laugh. After almost a fortnight he took her to a place where they could kiss without being seen. It wasn't long before she realised that he knew a lot of places where they could kiss without being seen.

Pretty girls started giving Aurora sideways glances.

The deaf girl, who they had never thought of as a threat, and who they had even felt sorry for, had inexplicably risen to become their rival. Aurora knew their love would be big news in their small town, and that before long everybody would know about it, even her grandmother. She decided to face the inevitable, and confess.

When the results had arrived confirming that the infant Aurora was profoundly deaf, her grandmother had known exactly what to do. Her parents being too busy with the five older children to find the extra time needed to care for a deaf child, she would take her in and raise her. Living just two streets away, the girl could see her family every day, and the old lady was prepared to devote as much time as it took to learning sign language. As she always seemed to know the right thing to do, a room in the house where she lived on her own was made ready.

She relished her granddaughter's every new trick and tantrum, and took to her sign lessons with enthusiasm. As the child learned, her grandmother was always a step ahead.

Every day Aurora joined her family for dinner. While they made every effort to include her in their chatter, none of them was as fluent as her grandmother. Outside school it was only with the old lady that she could make herself fully understood without having to write things down or point and mime, and in the intimacy of their conversation they became almost like sisters, confiding in one another, gossiping and evolving their own slang.

When she was small, Aurora had sometimes wept at the thought of the old lady dying, leaving her world a quieter, lonelier place. But as the girl grew up, her grandmother seemed to become more and more youthful, and for all her devotion to her granddaughter she still found the energy to stay in daily contact with her network of friends, who between them monitored the movements of everyone in the town and surrounding area. Even before the girl was really old enough to understand what she was being told, she became a repository for every piece of tittle-tattle that the old lady had heard or discovered. She felt as though she knew all there was to know about every unfortunate local character – about their unhappy marriages, their genito-urinary difficulties and their wayward children. And no matter how Aurora's vocabulary improved at school, her grandmother always kept pace. When she was fourteen, during a row about her new-found hobby of wearing too much make up, Aurora had signed an obscenity and found herself in as much trouble as if she had spoken the word. Where her grandmother had learned to understand such a terrible sign was a mystery to her, and although she continued to smuggle cheap cosmetics to school in her pencil case, this unusual flash of insolence left her truly ashamed and in even greater awe of her grandmother. She knew it wouldn't be long before the old lady found out about all the time she had been spending with the boy they had so often gossiped about.

'Grandmother,' she said. 'I've made a new friend.'

'I know.' She didn't look angry. 'I know you have, you poor girl.'

They talked across the kitchen table.

*　　　*　　　*

Aurora told her grandmother about how she and the boy had met, what they talked about, how he had promised to find a job, stop swearing and generally behave himself, of their dreams for the future and, of course, the depth of their love for one another. 'If you could meet him, grandmother, you would see how good-hearted he is, and that he isn't interested in stealing and fighting any more.'

'I'm sure he isn't. I'm sure he has suddenly become the best behaved boy in town, and it's all for the love of you.'

'Don't joke. When you meet him you'll see.'

'I'm not joking.' The old lady looked serious. 'I believe you.'

'Really? But why, after all the terrible things you've told me about him?'

The old woman shook her head, sighed, and gazed for a moment at her granddaughter. She knew that at this sight, where others would see a teenage girl like any other, this boy felt shivers, heard bells, and had difficulty fighting his tears of wonder. 'I always hoped it would be that pretty,

happy-go-lucky girl from the other side of town
– the one with the artificial left leg. But I suppose I always knew, deep down, that it would be
you – with your intelligence, your sweet, gentle
manner, and your dream of success outside this
small town.'

'Grandmother,' said Aurora, 'what are you talking about?'

'All this. You and that boy. You're both just
playing your parts in the oldest love story ever
told.' She shook her head. 'And there's nothing
anyone can do to stop it.'

The old woman explained. 'In every town in this
part of Italy the same story is played out generation
after generation. A gentle, bright, highly regarded
girl – just like you – meets the local savage and
falls wildly, hopelessly in love. It is always the least
likely girl, one who is very polite, a little shy, and
with something slightly . . . different about her.
Like you and your ears not working. It is always
the girl with the big birthmark across her face,
or the one whose elbows have been locked since

babyhood, really the last girl you would expect to begin a passionate romance with a notorious young criminal.' Aurora winced at this description of the boy she loved. 'Her love for him is so explosive, and so passionately reciprocated, that no one can separate them as they charge, half out of their minds, toward marriage.'

'So we'll be getting married?' she asked.

'Oh, maybe I'm wrong. Maybe your romance will be over before we know it. But I don't think so. For years the old people have been watching him with his light fingers, his drinking, his cursing, his snapping of car aerials and his urination on doorsteps and in flowerbeds, and watching you with your diligence at school and your quiet ambition in the face of your deafness. They've been waiting for this to happen for several years now, and it's happened right on cue. It was, I think, nineteen or twenty years since the last such episode in this town, and that's about the usual gap. I've always argued with them, saying, "No, look at this naughty boy, or that quiet girl," but I suppose that deep inside I've always known it would be you.

'Of course I found out straight away,' the old lady said. 'News reached me while you were sitting on that bench, scribbling love notes to one another.'

'But what happens to them once they are married?' asked Aurora. 'Will he get tired of me and go back to his old ways?'

'Oh no. These couples are always very happy together. He relinquishes his life of delinquency, they marry, have children and live and work like anyone else.'

'But what's so terrible about that? Why are you feeling so sorry for me?'

'Oh, nothing is *terrible* about it. It's just so . . . disappointing. For the girl's family.' The old woman closed her eyes, bit her lip and shook her head. 'Of course you realise you won't become a doctor now.'

'What? Why not?' Aurora was shocked. 'Why should this stop me?'

'Oh, it's just the way. You'll drift into domestic happiness and all the drive you feel to excel at university and in your profession will vanish. You'll be happy just being married, and will no longer feel the need to practise medicine.'

'But I can do both. I can love him and work too.'

'I am only telling you what I know. Remember, the story is old and it never changes. Sometimes, in a reflective moment, you will wonder how your life might have turned out had you never met him, but a smile from one of your children or an embrace from your husband will immediately banish such thoughts from your mind.'

'Well, we'll see about that,' said Aurora. The old woman reached across the table and touched her granddaughter's hand. 'But if your friends were so sure about all this, why did you never tell me?'

'Maybe I should have done. I suppose I was hoping that it was all just coincidence, or the foolish chatter of old gossips like me. But yes, I suppose if I had told you I would have extinguished the element of surprise. But it's too late now. You see, it always comes as a shock to the lovers. Neither spares the other a moment's romantic thought until suddenly they are living for one another. Without the surprise the story is not the story, and it is a story as old as the ground beneath our feet. And anyway,' she said, 'if I had told you I don't know what might have happened. It could have brought all kinds of bad luck. Maybe you would have done something stupid. You know I couldn't keep myself from warning you away from him, but all the girls in this town have been warned away from him. And sometimes it's best for people like me just to keep our mouths shut. You have no idea how difficult that was,' she said, 'but it's over now.'

Able at last to share these stories with Aurora, the old woman had never felt more like a fully-functioning grandmother. 'You see,' she began, 'a few years ago a pretty girl from Tarano took a meat cleaver and, one by one, sliced off all the fingers on her right hand in order to attract the attention of a boy who had been caught in the undertaker's, tearing gold teeth from the mouths of the corpses.'

'And did it work?' she asked. 'Did he fall in love with her?'

'No. Of course he didn't fall in love with her. This is what I mean. She had heard the story, probably from her talkative grandmother, and desperately wanted it to happen to her, but without the surprise of both lovers the story is not the story. Almost as soon as the boy was let out of jail he fell in love with a softly spoken, quietly intelligent girl who had been born without a single hair on her body. She enjoyed listening to and playing gentle piano music. Old men would linger outside her family's house as they passed, and listen as she played her Chopin or her Satie, or a delicate piece she had composed herself. *She hasn't got a hair on her*, they would whisper to one another as the music drifted into the street. *No eyelashes, nothing. She's as smooth as an egg all over. It's just as well she has her piano to console her because she'll never find a husband.* Before she met the tooth thief, quite by chance in a music shop where she was placing an order for the score of one of Toru Takemitsu's piano works, and he was trying to steal a trumpet, there was talk of her going to Milan to write atmospheric music for films and television.

They were married within three months, and have four children now.'

'Does she still play the piano?'

'Yes. But not with the same passion as before. She gives lessons to her children, and the children of her neighbours, but from what I'm told she no longer composes nor has any desire to compose.'

'But does this love always last, grandmother? Is it never just a passion that burns out in time?'

'It is always true, lasting love, and not just any old true love either. They shame the other married couples in the town with their devotion. The boy is absolutely ensnared by the girl. He spends his days thinking about her, worrying about her and working as hard as he can for her and for all their little children. And of course she is as devoted to him as he is to her, and gives her heart and soul to her husband. She bears his children and keeps his home comfortable, and does so quite happily and uncomplainingly. At first people shake their heads and sigh, and say to one another that it's a shame that what could have been a triumph on the girl's part over society's preconceptions and so on has been eclipsed by a very normal marriage. But before long people forget that she had been so full of promise, and he so wild and feared. Apart from their extraordinary devotion to one another they become a couple like any other – minding their own business, absorbed in their day to day lives, and taking pleasure in watching their children grow up happy and well-behaved.'

For the rest of the evening Aurora listened to her grandmother tell stories from their own town, and from Collevecchio and Forano and Vacone and Casperia, and even from as far away as Contigliano. While fascinated by the stories, she knew they didn't really apply to her, that although she had fallen for a reformed trouble-maker and would love him forever, she wouldn't allow herself to become trapped like the other girls. She saw herself reflected in their bottomless love for the formerly wayward men, and their desire to be the mother of their children, but she knew that she would never abandon her dream. She pictured herself in a few years time, rushing home from another successful operation to the waiting arms of her husband and the happy faces of their children. Aurora knew that her grandmother had no idea of the speed at which the world was changing, that the nature of love was unrecognisable from the way it had been just one or two generations before.

They talked until long past midnight. As the old woman kissed her granddaughter goodnight she knew that before long she would be pacifying the men in the family so that the young couple might quietly marry and continue playing their parts in the oldest love story ever told.

They filled notebooks, exercise books, ledger books and odd scraps of paper with their words. Every-thing, from their first conversation, was preserved – every revelation, every sad story or happy memory, and every banality. Words which for other couples would vanish almost immediately from memory were preserved as though they were museum pieces. If a conversation were to take place on a scrap of paper, that scrap would be saved, and stapled or pasted into the books. The only things they didn't write down were the words that didn't have to be said. Often they would go back and read their old writings, she playfully clipping his ear whenever, in an early conversation, they found a crossed-out expletive. They took turns in looking after the ever-growing pile of books.

He found work in his uncle's scrap yard, breaking and rebuilding old wrecks. He worked hard and learned fast, and his uncle was pleased with him as he patched cars together well enough for them to be sold. After a while he was allowed to live in a small cabin on the site. Among the car parts he dreamed of Aurora all day long – of her hair, her eyes and the things she did and said. She dreamed of him too – of his kisses and his handsome face. Her concentration evaporated, her marks plummeted and she was summoned, in disgrace, to the headmistress's office. She was struck with the realisation that all the hours she had previously spent studying she now spent talking about nothing much at all with her boyfriend, imagining their future together and, when she was absolutely sure nobody could see, letting him put his hand up her blouse.

'Well?' asked her headmistress.

'Yes. I'm sorry. I'll try harder. I'll make up for all the marks I've lost.' The headmistress doubted her sincerity.

On the bus home that afternoon Aurora worried that she really was becoming the girl in her grandmother's story. She had certainly spent enough time imagining herself with a baby on her hip, and living in a small but happy home with her devoted husband. That evening she saw her boyfriend, beat him at backgammon, kissed him, and let his fingers wander over her breasts. As had become routine, she brushed his hand away as it slid along the inside of her thigh. But she broke away from him earlier than she normally would have done, to sit in her room reading her schoolbooks, making notes and trying to steer her mind away from thoughts of love.

She didn't find it anywhere near as difficult as she thought she would.

The old lady had taken it upon herself to tell Aurora's parents about the romance. Their fury at the thought of their daughter's involvement with a well-known hooligan was softened by the old lady delightedly recounting example after example of the oldest love story ever told – tales from other towns, and from preceding generations in their own town. By the time they met him the boy was so hard-working, so well-behaved, and so obviously the boy in the old woman's stories that he immediately became a welcome visitor to their home, joining them for dinner almost every evening. They were happy for their poor, deaf daughter to have found a man guaranteed to love her and, however modestly, provide for her forever.

The boy spent hours talking to the old lady about other examples of his story. She seemed to have an endless supply. Hearing of how these boys felt new parts of their minds open when they met the girl, and how she had revealed to them a new sensitivity and intelligence that they had never known they had, he saw himself mirrored in every reformed tearaway – raised by reluctant uncles, disillusioned by school and drifting, as though it were the most natural thing in the world, into a life of petty crime. And in every unfortunate angel he saw Aurora. He and the old lady he had come to address as *grandmother* laughed at the girl's new-found enthusiasm for her studies, knowing that it was it was only a matter of time before she abandoned them for love. When they had laughed enough, they listed possible names for the children.

All the while, Aurora was studying hard. On the bus to and from school, and in bed at night, she pored over her textbooks, reading everything she was supposed to read and a lot more besides. In tests her marks returned to their previous levels, and images of herself at medical school and working intently on open hearts crept back into her mind. Every day she felt less like the girl in her grandmother's story.

One afternoon, when they had Aurora's grandmother's house to themselves, the young people rutted like dusty dogs driven wild by the summer heat. By the time the old lady came back from her social round, they were fully clothed and playing backgammon on the kitchen table. Smelling the sex in the air, she thought it would be best to start making concrete wedding plans straight away.

It had been Aurora's final attempt to feel love. The next day, as soon as he arrived at her house, she gave him the letter that she had spent all day writing and re-writing. She wanted to be there as he read it. He didn't cry. He didn't look at her. He just bit his bottom lip and went up into her bedroom, where he found the pile of books. Then he went away. She thought he had taken it very well, and hoped that in time they could be friends.

Back in his cabin he re-read all their conversations, starting with the first. On finishing each page he tore it out and set fire to a corner of it with the lighter that he hadn't used since he had given up smoking at Aurora's insistence. He watched their words burn until the fire hurt his fingers, then dropped the remaining scraps on to the floor and stamped out the flame with the sole of his boot. He was only part of the way through when his uncle came to start work. The boy started stripping the few remaining good parts out of a jeep that had rusted almost to nothing. In the early evening, as soon as his uncle was gone, he went back to his cabin, and the conversations. Page after page joined the pile of ash around his feet.

In the middle of the third night he burned the final page of their final conversation. He went into the yard and sat in the cab of an old truck, where he poured petrol over himself and, with romantic significance, lit the letter in which Aurora had told him that she had been doing a lot of thinking, that she was determined to go to medical school, that she couldn't realistically see them staying together for the rest of their lives, that if they were going to split up one day it might as well be sooner rather than later, that her grandmother had always been prone to flights of fancy, that the whole thing had been just another small town romance that was never going to work, and that having thought about it she realised that she had never really loved him.

Some said it was a miracle that he was found alive, and others said he would have been better off dead. Some said that God had saved him, others that he couldn't have used enough petrol, or that being in a closed truck cab must have stopped the flames from raging as they otherwise would have done. But without exception they talked and talked about how he was now a mess of burned flesh, how his clothes had melted and stuck to his raw skin, and how the flames had burned out his eyes, which was a blessing because at least he wouldn't be able to see himself looking the way he did. Without exception they blamed his girlfriend.

Months later, when they let him leave the hospital, he went back to his cabin. His uncle appointed him nightwatchman. His job was to sit outside and shout *Hey* at any sound that might possibly be an intruder. With nothing worth stealing in the yard he knew the job was his uncle's kindness in disguise. Occasionally he heard a clatter and shouted, but he knew it was just a cat, or his uncle rattling the gate to make sure he was earning his bed and board. Even if anyone had broken in, the human guard dog wouldn't have been able to do much about it. By the time he had raised himself up from his seat with the help of his stick and started to walk slowly in the direction of the noise, they would have taken whichever window winders or hubcaps or Michelin men had taken their fancy, and be long gone. Even so, he worked hard, listening to every sound the night threw in his direction. When it rained he wore a raincoat, and listened that little bit harder.

Every Tuesday afternoon he sat on their bench. At first his uncle led him there, but after a while he learned to make his way alone. Sometimes the old lady visited him. 'Hello grandmother,' he would say, recognising the shuffle of her footsteps and the waft of old lady smell as she sat beside him. He listened as she told him that his girl was sure to come back to him.

'She's bound to,' she would say. 'All this just

makes it a better story. It's so romantic, don't you think? With Aurora in her silent world, and you like this – all blind and burned to a cinder.'

She never gave him any news of the girl, and he never asked after her. She spoke only of their future together – the wedding day, their legions of little children, and how happy they would be. 'The story,' she said, 'will be told for miles around.'

'I know,' he said. When she had finished he said goodbye, and once, after she left, she never came back.

One Tuesday afternoon, when a light breeze was blowing and he could smell flowers but only guess at their colour, he felt Aurora's hand rest on his knee. 'Welcome home,' he whispered, even though he knew she couldn't hear him. He put his hand on hers. It was hairy and damp. It snuffled. It licked his hand and wrist. It whined. It was the muzzle of a dog, evidently hoping for something to eat. If he'd had a scrap of food in his pocket he would gladly have given it, but instead he pushed the dog away with his boot. He had known it wasn't her, but had happily drifted along with the delusion for a moment. He knew she wasn't coming back.

In fact he had found himself thinking about her less and less. At first he could think of nothing but Aurora and had missed her constantly, and when his uncle had arrived at work in the mornings he had gone into his cabin and cried his heart out over her. But, gradually, other girls from his past rose to rival her in his memory. He started to think that maybe she had been right to end their romance when she did, that they had too little in common to ever have had a long and happy marriage, that the old woman's story was a load of rubbish and that he would have been just as happy with any one of the pretty girls who had sucked him off behind the supermarket in the days before Aurora had come along. They were nice girls, good girls, and they would have made him get a job and stop stealing, and they would have settled down with him. With nothing much to prove they wouldn't have been set on going away to become doctors. With little to do but think about it, he concluded that Aurora hadn't saved him from his life of crime, not really. If he had fallen in love with anyone, which he was sure he would have done eventually, he would have calmed down and started to behave.

The dog made his way along the street, away from the man who did not give him any food. He started following a boy who was taking flamboyant drags on a stolen cigarette.

After a while the boy and the dog started walking towards a girl who was fiddling with her bicycle chain. It had come loose, and her fingers were black with oil. The cigarette thief recognised her as the girl who was famous all over town for having two sets of teeth. He had occasionally tried to glance inside her mouth as she walked past, but hadn't ever given her a great deal of thought. All he knew about her was that she kept herself to herself, was said to be exceptionally good at painting, and that nobody seemed to dislike her. He couldn't work out why his heart pounded as he approached her, why his mouth was suddenly so dry, why he felt so short of breath, or where the deafening sound of bells was coming from. Suddenly overwhelmed by the need to appear compassionate, and noticing the skinny dog at his heels, he reached into his pocket and took out a large stolen packet of wine gums. He tipped them on to the pavement. 'He looked hungry,' he said, trying to appear calm as he approached the girl, whose eyes had filled with wonder.

'What's his name?' she asked, with a catch in her voice.

'I don't know. He's not mine. But let's call him Giuseppe. Or,' he said, remembering her love of art, 'Leonardo da Vinci. Do you want a hand with your chain?'

Her fingers were trembling so much she had no chance of getting it back on. She had heard of this boy's shoplifting skill, and had been shocked at rumours of him drowning cats for fun. 'OK,' she said. She could hardly hear her own voice over the relentless crashing of the bells.

Giuseppe, or Leonardo da Vinci, ate all the wine gums as fast as he could. The static in the air was making his hair stand on end. Neither the boy nor the girl noticed when, his belly full of sugar, he ran north.

Cockroft liked to write poetry. He had once published a slim collection called *Sending Letter Bombs To Morris Dancers*. He had paid for it to be printed, and had been given a discount because some of the pages were upside down. It had sold four copies – one to his accountant, two to his daughter and another to Robin 'Red Breast' Robinson. They had all been offered copies for free, but had insisted on paying. He had kept two for himself, one to read and one for best, and sent the other four hundred and ninety-four to hospitals, prisons and public libraries, and to former friends, who he hoped would notice the veiled references to their treachery.

Believing he had said all he had to say, he had dramatically vowed never to publish again, but he still sometimes wrote the occasional verse. Sitting at the kitchen table while the Bosnian was, as usual, somewhere else, he picked up a chewed biro and found a sheet of paper. Inspired by the darkness outside, he wrote:

> *Timoleon Vieta, shining bright,*
> *In the forest of the night.*

He put the couplet in the ashtray and burned holes in it with his cigar, before setting fire to it with a match. When the flame had died he walked outside and stood in the dark, wondering what Timoleon Vieta might be up to. He no longer pictured him smiling as he chased cats around the pretty streets of Trastevere, or enjoying a discarded hamburger in the piazza by the Pantheon. Instead he saw the dog alone in a bad part of town – sad-eyed, emaciated and being chased away from dustbins by cleaver-wielding fat men in aprons. Sometimes he couldn't help picturing him dead, his body lying by the side of a busy road and rotting in the summer heat as cars roared by without stopping. In Cockroft's imagination a truck came along and, for fun, the driver squashed the dog flat beneath his enormous tyres. 'What have I done?'

he said, staring into the darkness. 'Oh, what have I done?'

He felt wretched. The night was still. 'Come home,' he shouted. He was surprised to hear an echo coming from somewhere. He felt as though his voice were bouncing around the whole of Italy, and that maybe the dog would hear him and do as he was told. 'Come home,' he shouted, as tears flooded down his cheeks, through his beard and on to his shirt. 'Timoleon Vieta, come home.'

The Bosnian could hear the old man from his room. He laughed until his sides hurt.

DUSTY

Timoleon Vieta carried on heading north, up hills and down hills. Baked by the heat he became wearier by the hour. Sometimes, when there was no water to be found, he had no choice but to lie in the shade during the day, only heading out when the sun started to go down. When he reached a river he would cool off, but only for as long as it took him to swim across the low, slow summer waters. Each day he became a little skinnier, and his paws more worn and broken, but he kept on going as quickly as he could. Heading, always, more or less north.

Lucia and Pietro married fairly young, and after thirteen years they had a baby girl. For a moment the midwife had thought the child was dead, strangled by the umbilical cord, but she soon showed signs of life. Not the wailing, struggling signs of life that Lucia had been told to expect, but almost inaudible sobs. She was rushed to another part of the hospital. Later, the doctor told Lucia and Pietro that their daughter's mind was unlikely ever to develop beyond babyhood.

When they were finally allowed to take her home they couldn't take their eyes from her. Sometimes, as Lucia fed her and looked down at her puckered mouth and fat cheeks, it almost seemed as if nothing was wrong.

Pietro went back to work, and Lucia stayed at home, where she tried to teach things to the girl, who they had named Rosa. There were people who said it was hopeless, that it would have been better for everyone if she had not survived.

Rosa slept in her parents' room at the front of the house, which was quite big and had lots of light coming in through the window. When she was a bit older Lucia and Pietro let her stay there while they moved into the small room at the back of the house.

At the age of four she was the size of any four-year-old, and had long, thick hair, but she couldn't bring a spoon to her mouth and she couldn't stand up without someone holding on to her. Unlike some of their older relatives, Lucia had never bothered praying for a miracle, but she spent every moment she could paying close attention to her daughter, trying to stimulate her and hoping for tiny signs of progress.

It was hard to tell whether Rosa even knew where she was, or what was going on around her. Doctors said she wasn't blind, but her eyes didn't seem to be focusing on anything, and sometimes Lucia came close to giving up hope of her ever reacting or doing anything new. Then one morning, at about twenty past ten, Lucia stood her daughter on her feet and held on to her, as she had done so many times before. Slowly, she let go. Instead of tipping backwards or to the left, as she had always done before, Rosa stayed still.

She wobbled, but stayed upright for about half a minute before toppling backwards to be caught by her mother's waiting hand.

When Pietro came home he found his wife wild with excitement. Desperate to see the trick with his own eyes, he asked Lucia to try it again. Thinking it must have been a fluke of balance, he was amazed to see his daughter standing upright unsupported.

Within a fortnight, with her mother holding both her hands, she was making faltering steps.

To the bemusement of the staff and the parents of the other children, when Rosa was seven Lucia and Pietro enrolled her in the local school. They argued that she was a child like any other, and should therefore go to school. She was allowed a trial period of a fortnight, after which the headmaster expected to be able to declare her presence disruptive, and recommend she remain at home or be transferred to a special school. On her first day she was dressed in her uniform and guided to a desk at the back of the classroom. She sat in her seat, sometimes slumping forward and sometimes sitting back in an uncomfortable-looking position. The seat beside her, in the back corner of the room, was kept empty, but if one of the other children was misbehaving they would be told to go and sit next to Rosa. As they were unable to make mischief with her, the class would continue calmly. She became popular with her teacher.

During breaks, while the other children were playing outside, Lucia came to look after her. The other girls from her class started to linger and watch, wide-eyed, as Rosa was helped to the toilet and fed spoonfuls of mashed-up food. She reminded them of a doll, and they asked if they could help. They already had a tortoise, and now they had Rosa too.

Other girls joined in, and soon they became so familiar with the routine, and so indifferent to the messiness of it all, that they could look after her on their own. As long as Lucia was around to make sure everything was going smoothly, they could be left to it. Some of the girls' mothers, worried by the stories their daughters were bringing home, came to see what was going on, and found themselves as absorbed by the strange rituals as their children were. They ended up offering to help out, and Lucia no longer needed to visit her daughter every day, and was free to take on odds and ends of work. In the mornings she dropped Rosa off at the school gate with her food in plastic pots, and whichever girls had been appointed her guardians for the day rushed up and fussed around her, guiding her towards the classroom, where she sat beside the empty chair that was still reserved for troublemakers, until it was time to go outside. Once everyone was sure she was clean and comfortable, she sat quietly in the shade as the other children ran around, shouting their lungs out.

Pietro's grandmother had flown into a frenzy of excitement at the news of the pregnancy, and this frenzy had turned into hysteria on being told that her first great-grandchild would never really stop being a baby. She became a frequent visitor to the house. At every opportunity the old woman told people how she pitied her great-granddaughter, and how she prayed for her as often as she could. She filled her house with photographs of the girl. There was something slightly different about Rosa in each one. She was dressed in different clothes, or wearing her long hair in a different way, but her face hardly changed – her eyes seeming not to be focused on anything, and her mouth slightly open.

One evening, when Rosa was nine, her great-grandmother came to the house to look after her while Lucia and Pietro were out. She sat by her bedside, singing sentimental songs. Her thin voice drifted through the air and out into the front yard. Halfway through a song, Rosa's eyes began to shine, and seemed to look around the room, taking in details as though she were seeing them for the first time. They settled for a moment on her great-grandmother's face. The girl started to laugh, a child's giggle, her shoulders shaking. The old woman had no idea how long this lasted, but it wasn't long before Rosa returned to her normal self, quietly lying on her bed, her eyes seeming not to see anything, and her mouth slightly open and shapeless, as if she had never smiled at all. The old woman became convinced that Rosa would soon be making a full recovery.

A few weeks later Lucia arrived at the school to collect Rosa, and found everyone in a state of excitement. Unable to make much sense of the chorus of ecstatic children helping her daughter along, she asked their teacher why they were so excited.

'Oh, Rosa smiled in class,' she said. 'We were learning about volcanoes, and this giggle came from the back of the room. Everyone turned to look, and there she was, smiling and laughing and looking at us all, one by one. It must have lasted for about half a minute before she sat back in her seat as if nothing had happened. The children gave her a round of applause. That was this morning, and they haven't calmed down since. They keep expecting her to do it again. How often does she do it?'

'Not very often.' Lucia had thought the old

woman's story had been the result of some kind of religious frenzy, or the onset of dementia. 'Not very often at all.'

Lucia and Pietro talked until two in the morning about how much they wanted to see their daughter smile. Just once, they said. If they could just see her smile it would make them happy for the rest of their lives.

Zeno's father had something to do with ball bearings. Because of this he moved to a new town every few weeks, taking his wife and son with him. Zeno could never quite understand why his father couldn't just work in one place, but he had stopped asking a long time before he arrived in Todi, shortly before his tenth birthday. It was his seventeenth school.

The first day at a new school had long since ceased to be nerve-racking, and had become a routine as predictable as any other. His father would give him a pocket full of ball bearings, and drop him off a couple of hundred metres from the gate. Within minutes of entering any school he knew who the nasty kids were, which ones would never be a threat, and roughly where he would slot into the pecking order. It was always somewhere near the bottom.

He had never known anyone who didn't like ball bearings, who didn't enjoy looking at them, secretly rolling them around their palms during lessons and, in the yard, sending them speeding along the ground, where they lost their lustre but gained battle scars.

On his first morning at every school he was ignored in the classroom, apart from occasional suspicious glances. Sometimes somebody would be told that it was their job to be friendly to him, but they never tried too hard. When they were let out into the yard he always stood alone in an identifiably neutral spot as the other children kept themselves at a distance. He tried to avoid eye contact with anyone lower down the order than he was. The last thing he needed was to be associated with the gentler, more pleasant children until he had made peace with the ones who, if they wanted to, could make his every day a nightmare. When he was inevitably approached and sized up by a hard-faced kid, he would make mention of his ball bearing connection at the earliest opportunity, and offer one as a gift. Unable to refuse, his potential tormentor was always caught off-guard. Soon, word of free ball bearings spread among the rough boys. As they busied themselves racing them down slopes or throwing them at each other's teeth, they started to think that maybe the new kid wasn't so bad after all. He was always careful to save the biggest ball for the toughest boy in the school, and by the end of the day he was safe to blend into the background, where he would remain until the day he came home to be told by his father to put his things in boxes because in the morning they would be moving to a town just far away enough for him to be mocked for using the slang he had only just got the hang of.

At a school in Boveglio, Zeno had encountered a particularly difficult bully who, at the end of the first day, had demanded he empty his pockets and hand over every ball bearing he had left. 'I bet you don't know how they make them,' Zeno had said, as he handed them over. 'I bet you don't know how they get them so round.'

'Of course I know,' said the bully, and took his spoils home. The next morning the bully was waiting for him, his brow furrowed. He quietly asked Zeno to tell him how they were made. 'I do know,' he said. 'I've just forgotten.' Zeno explained, and was never bothered again.

At a school in Faenza, his father had neglected to give him any ball bearings on his first day, and he had suffered seven weeks of name-calling and threats.

And so it was with a pocket full of currency and a mind poised to explain the horrors and the wonders of the bearing works that he stood in the Todi schoolyard. People weren't paying him much attention at all. They were just going about their business. He leaned against a wall and looked at the new faces, wondering which of them would, for a while, become his friends. He always hooked up with a small group of people in the end. He never kept in touch with them after he left town, but it was good to have some people to hang around with.

He noticed a group of girls holding on to the simple girl he had seen sitting at the back of his class. They guided her into a chair in the shade, and left her alone. He watched her as her head flopped forwards, and swung slowly from side to side. She clearly didn't know what was going on, and he couldn't work out why she went to school at all. She didn't even have any pens or pencils, and he wondered why she didn't just stay at home. He looked around to confirm that he was still being disregarded, and dug into his pocket for one of the smaller ball bearings. He threw it, underarm, at the stupid girl. He missed. Nobody had noticed, so he tried another and scored a direct hit on the top of her head, which flew up before flopping back into its original position. A third ball hit her cheek, and secured a similar response. Desperate to impress the tough-looking boys who were standing a little way away and proving so indifferent, he called over to them. 'Hey,' he shouted. 'Look at this.'

He selected a medium-sized ball, and threw it. It hit her shoulder, and she jumped at the shock. He quickly followed his direct hit with another.

She jumped again, this time letting out a sharp cry. The boys moved towards him. Seeing that he had attracted their attention he reached into his pocket for another ball. He was going to offer it to one of them to throw at the girl.

Before he had had a chance to offer it he had been knocked to the ground, and was being kicked from every angle. Each kick was fuelled by the purest love for Rosa. To see her tormented was more than the boys could bear, and even as they raged they had difficulty holding back their tears.

Having heard whispers of Rosa being picked on, all the children gathered around to watch the kicking. Nobody cheered or became hysterical as they usually did when a fight broke out. They just watched the new boy get kicked, and listened to his appeals for mercy and his apologies. Some of the girls left the crowd to put their arms around Rosa. They shouted that she was fine, that she wasn't crying or anything, and the kicks slowed down. By the time a teacher arrived, Zeno had lost a tooth and was red with bruises.

The bruises turned purple, then green, and faded in time. He found a small group of friends and settled into a fairly normal school life. His crime was soon more or less forgotten, but sometimes his new friends reminded him of his first day. 'Do you remember what you did with those ball bearings?' they asked. 'Do you remember throwing them at Rosa? Do you remember being kicked in?'

'Yes,' he would say, burning with shame at having tormented the girl. 'Yes, I remember.'

After about three months he left Todi for Priverno. For the first time he decided to stay in touch with somebody from an old town. Whenever he moved to a new town he would send Rosa a postcard, care of the school, describing his new town and wishing her well. He didn't know why he wrote the postcards. He just did. As they reached her home her parents would hold them in front of her, and read the message. After he had sent her about half a dozen they collected all the postcards she had ever been sent, and put them in an album.

*   *   *

Rosa's album grew and grew, and Lucia often sat with her as she lay propped up on her bed, turning its pages and commenting on the pictures and what her friends had written. They were in clear plastic pockets so it was possible to see both sides. Reading these familiar messages to her daughter, she was moved by the love they all contained. Knowing she couldn't read, and couldn't understand the words when they were read to her, Rosa's friends still wrote detailed greetings from distant places, telling her of the fun they had been having on holiday and wishing her well. Girls ended their postcards with showers of kisses, and boys with a *see you soon*.

'Look at that, Rosa,' she said to her one day, pointing at a picture of the Golden Staircase at the Palazzo Ducale in Venice. Rosa seemed to focus on the picture, taking in all the details. She smiled, and broke into a laugh, punctuated with excited gasps. She sat up, and looked at her mother. Their eyes met. Lucia touched her daughter's cheek. Rosa started laughing again as though her mother were the funniest thing she had ever seen. Then her eyes lost their sparkle, her mouth lost its shape and she fell back on to her pillows.

The doctor had told them that this kind of episode was probably just something to do with her nervous system, but Lucia now knew for sure that he didn't know what he was talking about. If he could see her like this he would be amazed, and would probably start crying too.

Pietro came home, and his wife rushed to meet him. 'If only you had come home five minutes ago,' she said.

It became clear to everyone how pretty Rosa would have been. She would have broken the hearts of romantic boys. But despite her long, lustrous hair and luxuriant figure, her vacant expression, lolling head and sudden, apparently pointless movements were the same as they had always been.

Sometimes somebody who was new to the area would pass by the house, see her sitting in the front yard and fall desperately in love with a glimpse of her perfect skin or her shining hair. When, on a subsequent walk past the house, dressed in his best clothes, the man saw her gaping mouth and her eyes that didn't seem to be looking in any particular direction, he would rush away as his vision of the future collapsed. Lucia and Pietro made a game of looking out for these men. They called them Rosa's husbands.

After she left school she received a stream of visitors. Girls came in the evenings to sit beside her in the fresh air, hug her, read her magazine gossip columns and true stories of ordinary Italians doing extraordinary things, arrange her hair in elaborate and experimental styles, and tell her secrets they had promised to keep. Boys, always in twos or threes, sat beside her, usually silent but occasionally commenting on the weather or something that was happening in the street. Sometimes when there was a party she would be dressed up nicely, placed in a comfortable chair and looked after.

Shortly after she was born Lucia and Pietro had been told that it was only a matter of time before Rosa died, that she would always be weak and susceptible to any illnesses that happened to be going around, and that one day one of them would finish her off. It could be next week, the doctor had said, or it could be in a while. Either way, she would never be an old lady.

For all their unwillingness to accept what they had been told, they couldn't help noticing that whenever their daughter caught a cold it seemed to go on forever, and when her stomach was in turmoil she wept with the pain of it, sometimes for days on end. The older she got, the more protracted her illnesses became.

The doctor always tried his best for her and remained as optimistic as he could, even in the face of her worst periods of ill health. But, at last, she became so ill that he knew she wasn't going to get better, that she would be unlikely to see her twentieth birthday. He told Lucia and Pietro that if they wanted to they could put her in a hospital in another part of town, but that it would do her no good. They decided to keep her at home, where she could lie in her bed with the window open to the clean, fresh air, with photographs of her friends on the wall and music playing quietly on the radio.

They were determined for her not to die alone. Their bosses, who knew Rosa well, allowed them to arrange their shifts so that she would always have one of them by her side, stroking her hair or holding her hand. The thought of her dying without being directly and passionately adored was too much to bear. So it was with eyes on her every minute of the day and night that she grew weak, thin and pale, and her breathing became irregular. She had to be carried to the bathroom. Friends visited her every evening, under strict instructions not to start crying until they had left the room. And all the while, as they huddled around her, one or other of Rosa's parents stayed in the room, their eyes fixed on their daughter. If one of her friends stood in the way they moved to somewhere they could get a clear view of her. Pietro never stopped hoping that, just once, he would see Rosa smile. He couldn't stop thinking of Lucia's description of what she had seen. Ever since hearing it he had nurtured an image of her laughing, her eyes alight and full of love.

*   *   *

On a still, scorching Tuesday afternoon, when Lucia was at work and Pietro was watching over Rosa with his hand pressed on hers, the whine of a starving stray burst into the room through the open window, obliterating the peace. He thought the dog would go away if he ignored it, but after a few relentless minutes it seemed as though it would stay there forever, singing its ugly song. Worried that the whines and yelps would disturb his daughter, whose brow had puckered into a slight frown, he walked to the window and leaned out. The dog was a dirty thing with xylophone ribs. Pietro bared his teeth and quietly growled at it. It ran away.

Returning to Rosa's bedside, Pietro stroked her hair as it lay on the pillow. Her eyes were closed, and her breathing almost inaudible. After a while the dog returned, and continued its whining. Pietro went back to the window and leaned out. Again he bared his teeth and quietly growled, but this time the dog didn't run away. It stayed there, emaciated and yelping. He kicked off his left shoe, and threw it. He missed the dog, and it shuffled a short way away. He kicked off his right shoe, and threw it hard. This time the heel clipped the dog's muzzle, which rang like a woodblock. With a final yelp it ran away, its tail between its legs.

Pietro returned once more to Rosa's bedside to find her silent, her eyes closed and her mouth wide open. Nobody had been there to watch over her, to hold her hand, to kiss her forehead, or to whisper words of love.

Pietro never told Lucia about the dog. He told her he had been at their daughter's side and that in her final moments she had looked more peaceful than he had ever seen her before.

He never forgot the way the dog had taken him away from her. He couldn't stop replaying the scene in his mind, but no matter how infuriated he was by the memory of the dog's intrusion into his life, there was something about him that he couldn't help but pity. He remembered the dog's eyes, the way they had pleaded so desperately as he looked up at the window. The more he thought about those eyes, the more unreal the whole scene seemed to become. He was sure his memory had made them more beautiful than they could possibly have been.

He drifted into reveries about what might have happened if things had been different when the dog had arrived. He and Lucia would have been pleased to see him, and would happily have given him food. They would have sat Rosa in the yard and placed her hand on his back, and watched as her fingers scrunched his fur. Not having the heart to send him back into the world, they would have kept him as a pet – feeding him up, washing his coat, and calling him *Dusty* so he never forgot how lucky he was to have found them. He saw all four of them, laughing in the sun.

Cockroft spent most of his time wishing his life had been different. He wished he hadn't lost his way on that television programme. He wished he had stuck with his original stage name, Dudley Salterton, or not changed his name at all. There was nothing wrong with the name David. Everything was wrong with the name Carthusians. He couldn't even remember what it meant, or why he had chosen it. But he had stuck with it, hoping it would bring him luck as it had seemed to at first, because within two weeks of becoming Carthusians Cockroft he had made his first appearance on television, and had fallen hopelessly in love with Monty 'Misty' Moore, a struggling pianist who moved into his flat two days after their first meeting. For a while Cockroft had enjoyed the most productive period of his life. Tunes poured out of him and he shared them joyfully with his handsome new friend, who learned them all note for note. He also wished the boy in the silver shorts had never left him. He wished Robin 'Red Breast' Robinson hadn't died. He wished he had never married that poor, nervous girl, and he wished he hadn't been a relatively bright child. He had been plucked from his primary school after accidentally winning a scholarship to a nearby public school, where he spent years among boys who believed they ruled the world, as some of them did in their way. Boys who would inherit swathes of Rhodesia, or become fat and lazy MPs. Boys who despised him for being a child from those ugly new houses in the next town, and whose parents silently resented his presence at such an expensive school because they wanted to keep their Cecils, their Clives and their St. Johns away from boys who lived in ugly new houses. Even the more pleasant boys, and there were a few, the ones who missed their mothers and didn't throw their weight around, left him alone. They didn't know how to talk to him, and couldn't really see the point in trying. To make things worse he was always near the bottom of the class. His teachers loathed him and tormented him for having so obviously simply had a good day when he sat his scholarship exam. The only subject he excelled at was music, which was the real reason why the school had admitted him after reading his pedestrian exam papers. He got on well with his teacher, who would invite him into the music room during breaks and after school and let him play any instrument he liked. Once, when Cockroft was fourteen, he and his teacher, an amiable married man of forty-eight, had spent fifteen minutes kissing in the xylophone cupboard. Occasional fumbles had followed. They always ended with the teacher begging Cockroft never to tell anybody, which he never did, and running shamefaced from the cupboard. Cockroft supposed he must be dead by now.

Every day Cockroft had gone back to his family, leaving the other boys to do the things he wanted to do more than anything in the world. For as much as he feared the nasty boys, he desperately wanted them to come to him silently in the night and fuck him until his arse was raw, and to take him in their arms and kiss him because they loved him more than they could ever have imagined. But he took the bus home late every afternoon, back to his mother and father, and spent most of his evenings alone in his room, or playing the piano and violin they had saved so hard for. He could only guess at what went on in the dormitories after lights out, and he guessed for hours and hours. A miserable beast with one back, he pictured moonlit pools of writhing limbs.

He wished he could have gone to the normal school like the other children in his street, the children who, quite rightly, mocked his absurd uniform as he walked to and from the bus stop.

Then maybe, he told himself, he wouldn't have spent most of his life trying so desperately to be accepted by people with far too much money, and chasing after men with far too many names, men who would never dream of leaving their wives to move in with him.

'It was terrible,' he mumbled to the Bosnian, who was sitting in the deckchair next to him and staring into the distance without a word. 'They hated me. I could never join in with them. There were two other scholarship boys in my year and they were both good at rugby and cricket and things like that, so everyone put up with them. They didn't put up with me though. Pale, musical, uncoordinated, quiet old me. I was always the outsider, shunned all day and going home every night to his ordinary little house and his ordinary little mother and father.' He sighed, shook his head and drained his glass of wine. 'There were no games of spunky biscuit for Cockroft.'

The Bosnian had played spunky biscuit plenty of times, and had tormented quite a few scholarship boys too, taunting them with his future of certain wealth and laziness. An easy, well-paid job in a family friend's firm in the City, a legacy or two and help from the family purse. He had never quite been able to forgive his father for losing almost everything in an insurance gamble gone wrong. He had been fourteen when it had happened. Frantic to keep their boy away from state school, and not particularly wanting him around the house during term time, his family pulled in all their resources and somehow managed to cover his school fees, but he realised with horror that if he was going to get his hands on even half the stuff he wanted in the outside world then he would have to work almost as hard as an ordinary person. His father had been forced to sell his flat in London, the place in St. John's Wood where it had long been accepted that the Bosnian was going to live for free while he was establishing himself in town. Now he would have to pay rent like ordinary people, and this would mean having to think about money, and having to hand over chunks of whatever he earned to a complete stranger. His blood went cold at the thought. But, at sixteen, he found a partial solution. Even if he did have to make a living, he was determined not to break a sweat.

He started his apprenticeship, draining the enormous disposable incomes of his fellow pupils by dealing grass and ecstasy. He tried selling speed and LSD at first, but they never really caught on (apart from with a couple of *Dark Side Of The Moon* fans who went for the occasional tab of acid) because they were deemed by most of his customers to be for povs and New Age scum respectively. Before long he realised where the real money was, and cocaine became his main source of income. He bought it from a local dealer, and sold it very discreetly to the more adventurous boys for twice what he had paid for it. It was easy, and he was never caught. When he went to an old university he carried on, selling to the moneyed boys and girls who could afford the coke but were frightened of going to real dealers, and when he graduated he moved down to London and set himself up as a gentleman's powder peddler, somebody expensive but safe and discreet. He was very popular. Pretty girls went out of their way to have sex with him.

He worked two or three days a week on a friend's lifestyle magazine, where he did very little. He didn't need the money but the job enabled him to tell his family he was working, and made him look legitimate to the tax man. It also gave him an excuse to move in the kind of circles where people sniffed as much cocaine as they could get their hands on. Without the golden egg he had been expecting, he chipped away at the golden eggs of other people, people whose fathers hadn't lost most of their money, who were falling over themselves to spend their largely unearned incomes on getting off their faces in the most extravagant ways they could. London was full of them, and he followed them around to places like Cowes, where he could clear seven or eight grand in a week without even trying as they partied between yacht races, always celebrating when he got back to London with a long weekend of champagne and whores.

At one point he decided to become a little more businesslike, and changed suppliers. Caught up in a row with his old supplier, he ended up being shot in the arm in a barn somewhere in Essex. Too scared to go to hospital he drove home, grabbed his passport, four thousand pounds in cash and a bag full of clothes, and got a friend to drive him to Dover as he wrapped expensive shirts around his arm. The shot, which had been surprisingly quiet, had made a deep graze, but the blood stopped after a while. When he arrived in France he took a train to Italy, because that was where his family had often gone on holiday, first to the apartment on the Riviera that they had been obliged to sell, and then to friends' villas here and there. He knew enough of the language to get by.

That had been a year and a half before. He had his head shaved, and took to wearing scruffy clothes as a disguise. It had taken him only a few days to realise that by doing a bad impersonation of a suicidal Björn Ulvæus he could easily pass as a Bosnian and live from the sympathy of pretty girls doing Europe or, in this case, the sympathy of a stupid, boring old man. When he discreetly confided his Balkan history to people he found that that nobody seemed to know anything about Bosnia, except that it was a terrible place to come from, and that everyone who had escaped from it having been shot in the arm deserved sympathy, patience and, if it was in any way possible, sex. Still, to be sure, he avoided anybody who looked as though they might know anything about Balkan affairs. There were very few people who did, only the occasional grey-templed man in a light linen suit.

Once a month he called his mother, telling her he was teaching English, or working in a hotel kitchen to improve his Italian, and that he would be returning home before long. He had no difficulty reeling off stolen anecdotes about eccentric students and psychotic chefs. She listened, disinterestedly. 'How Bohemian,' she would say, not really knowing what that meant, or 'How Orwellian,' even though she had never read Orwell. He always let the money run out mid-sentence. She never asked him exactly when he would be coming home. She didn't seem too bothered, and anyway he didn't know. She occasionally gave him news of his sisters, but they were off at boarding school and university most of the time so she really had no idea what they were up to, and had very little to say about them.

He was still scared of those people from Essex. He had bad dreams about them. He didn't even feel safe in Italy, not really. He kept imagining them coming after him, tracking him down and finishing off the job as a matter of pride, as they said they were going to do as he had run bleeding from the barn. They had told him he was in way out of his depth, and they had been right. He moved around as much as he could, but he always felt he was going to run into somebody he knew, which could obliterate his cover. He had been driven into the crotch of the old man by two chance meetings with friends of his family in the space of three days as he walked around Florence, a traditional place for him to meet girls. He had fobbed them off with tales tying in with the lies he had told his mother, in case these sightings were reported back at home, and swiftly turned the conversation to the Duomo. But he had been frightened. Having watched a lot of films in which people were chased across the world by vengeful criminals, he had panicked. Going home was too risky, and going to a country where he didn't know the language and where it was less credible for a Bosnian to be stealthily wandering around would have been too much of a leap into the unknown. He was afraid of dying, and the old man had provided him with a safe option.

As with his dealing, he considered the time he had spent with the old man to have been a kind of victory. He thought about how hard other people had to work to get by. All his life he had scoffed at people with ordinary jobs, and in a few minutes each week he saved days of washing dishes, driving vans, teaching English to Italians, pushing a pen, moving boxes around in a room with no windows, selling cogs, or doing whatever it was that people who worked actually did so they could pay the rent and buy food and pay the bills. His job wasn't hard to do, which is why he had accepted the deal so readily when the old man had offered it to him. It was easy and straightforward, and he had supposed it wouldn't be much different from losing a game of spunky biscuit. He didn't know. He had never lost a game of spunky biscuit. Whatever, it beat working. But he had begun to think about moving on. Even though he didn't want to die, he had started thinking more and more about home.

Timoleon Vieta was almost home. He walked with his tail in the air and his raw feet moving quickly along the road leading to the turning to his master's house. His body ached, but soon he would be home – sitting at his master's feet, being stroked and eating from a big bowl of food.

A van pulled up beside him. Some people got out and started to pet him and give him scraps of food. They put some pieces of dry bread on the floor of the van, and he jumped up to eat them. The sliding door slammed shut and the people drove north, happy to have a new pet.

HENRI

One of them opened the sliding door. He put his hand over his nose and mouth, and mumbled, 'Fuck.' The turd was a neat coil, like a plastic toy, and the air was thick with the taste of it. He called the dog, who jumped down from the van.

'Now fuck off,' he said, pointing. The dog moved away, his tail between his legs and his skinny belly almost scraping along the ground. The man followed, shooing him along and telling him to fuck off until he was a long way from the van. He walked back to the camper, checking over his shoulder to make sure the dog wasn't following him. He wasn't. He was walking away, along the road that ran in to the town.

They all stood beside the van, looking in through the open door. None of them knew what to do next. None of them had ever had to clean up dog shit before.

Timoleon Vieta walked fast through the streets of Pisa. Some people didn't notice him, some ignored him, and others cursed him as he bumped into their legs. He changed direction several times, and at one point he was almost run over by an ancient Ape 50 carrying a cargo of flowers. Then he stopped, and sat in the shadow of a small church. Two people walked by, carrying the scent of food. He left the shade and followed them along. It wasn't long before he was being scratched behind his ears, eating the crisps that had caught his attention, and being spoken to in words that came from France, and from Cambodia, and from the Italian phrase book in the dentist's bag.

Malic was crouching in the shade under the house, her arms immersed to the elbows in a bowl of washing, when she saw Sophal coming in her direction. He was leading one of his father's buffalo. The creature was docile, and Sophal was holding on to the slack rope with his right hand while dragging his stick along the ground with his left. Malic's heart jumped at the sight of the boy, as it had begun to every time she saw him, and she rushed up the wooden stairway and into the house before he had a chance to see her. She busied herself with a broom, not wanting her mother to come home and find her idle with a half-finished load of washing on the ground. She swept frantically, trying hard to put so much concentration into the act that she would stop thinking about Sophal, about how tall he had grown, and how handsome. It didn't really work. Knowing he was so near, she trembled and kept dropping the broom.

In her memories Sophal was just her older brother Panarith's best friend. The boys had been inseparable, and Sophal had often played in or around their house. Although she was never invited, she often joined in their games. Sometimes they were content to play around the neighbourhood with the other children or, after the rain, to stay in the back yard sculpting replicas of Angkor Wat from the soft, damp earth. On other days, often on Malic's initiative, they had adventures that took them away for hours on end along dusty tracks, into rice fields and sometimes as far as the next village. As she always seemed to be the one who had the good ideas, neither boy complained about Panarith's little sister tagging along with them.

Their favourite thing was to paddle Sophal's uncle's boat along the river, dragging fishing hooks behind them and collecting driftwood as it floated by. When they arrived home with armfuls of damp sticks, and plastic bags full of water and live, struggling fish, Malic and Panarith were given praise for being good children. If they were lucky, they were rewarded with a coconut from the garden or a stick of sugar cane, which they would enjoy all the more in the knowledge that they were being treated for nothing more than having been on an adventure.

In those days Sophal had been just another boy, a friend to have fun with. Now, with him being sixteen and having to work on his father's farm all the time, and with Malic helping her mother around the house and running errands for her father, they only ever saw each other in passing. It was only since she had turned fourteen that he had begun to upset her with his smile, his faultless skin, his clear eyes and his wiry body. Just a short while previously she would have waved at him as he passed and they would have had a short, shouted conversation. She might even have walked along with him for a while.

When she was sure he would be out of sight she put down the broom and went back underneath the house to continue her washing. It was getting dark by the time she had finished hanging the clothes on the line that was strung between two of the stilts, and the frogs were coming out.

Her mother had returned and was getting the evening meal ready, her father had come in from his motorcycle repair workshop next to their house and was wiping the oil from his fingers, and her grandmother was awake and coughing. Malic was called upstairs to eat.

After the meal, while everyone else was watching the small television set that was attached to an old truck battery, Malic went to the curtained-off corner of the room that she shared with her grandmother and, without thinking, switched on her reading light and reached for a thick photo album. On the front was written, in French and Khmer, *Morakot In Europe*. She knew every detail of these pictures, and knew by heart every word of the commentary she had written next to each one, but she still looked at them every day. Her sister was in every photograph, usually standing in front of a famous landmark. Malic knew the photographs so well that she didn't pay much attention to whatever it was that was supposed to be the focus of the picture. When she looked at Morakot in front of the palace in London, she no longer thought too much about the soldiers in their ridiculous hats, or the flag that told everyone that the Queen was at home. Instead she tended to look at the man who had wandered into the left-hand side of the shot and was standing some way behind Morakot. He was fatter than anyone she had ever seen, and his eyes were bulging so far out of his face that it seemed as though they were about to pop out and roll along the ground. In the photograph where Morakot was standing on the bank of Lake Geneva in what looked like the biggest coat in the world, in the background a bicycle with a buckled wheel was lying on its side. Although her sister had written to her about the snow in the mountains, the chocolate, and the cuckoo clocks that rich people travelled across the world to buy, whenever Malic thought of Switzerland she thought of it as a land of broken bicycles.

She had spent so many hours looking at these photographs that she almost felt she had been to the places herself, that she had seen the car with the dented door by the Arc de Triomphe, and the friendly dog by the falling-down tower in Italy. But what she liked most of all about these photos was their one constant – her sister. She was always there, usually wearing thick clothes to keep out the cold – big wooly hats, gloves and jackets. Malic had been used to seeing her wearing a sarong, and took a while to adjust to the sight of her in jeans. But once she had got used to the difference she decided that her sister's new clothes suited her very well. In every photograph she looked more beautiful than the places where she stood, which Malic had been told were very famous.

Some of the photographs had been taken by other tourists. In these her husband was by her side, looking either directly into the camera or at his wife with eyes that, to Malic, seemed to be burning with love.

As usual, her grandmother stumbled through the gap between the curtains and under her mosquito net, and flopped on to the mattress that had been assembled from various odd pieces of foam. She was bald and toothless and did little apart from eating, sleeping and making noises, but Malic was happy to share her part of the room with her. She could still walk a short way, and would sometimes lie in her hammock in the shade under the house, where she immediately fell asleep, her snores resounding through the street. Malic liked to rock her like a baby.

Sometimes, though, the old woman would shake

Malic awake in the middle of the night to whisper stories to her as though they were urgent information. 'You know, I am a thousand years old,' she would say, her lips smacking against her gums. Malic found this funny, and never minded being woken up. 'I have done so many things. Once I even presented a basket of durians to King Jayervarman VII.' The old woman chuckled at the memory. 'He liked me, I could tell. I was every bit as beautiful as your sister Morakot back then, you know, and as beautiful as you will be one day.'

When Francois announced that he was going to Phnom Penh for a year, everyone teased him. 'So,' they all said, laughing at their wit. 'I suppose you'll be coming back with a Cambodian wife.'

'Just the one?' he would reply, smiling through the tedium. 'I'll be bringing at least three back with me. You wait and see.'

The only person who didn't tease him was his fiancée. She admired his compassion, and knew he would be working hard, writing to her regularly and behaving himself very well. And he did. On weekends he sometimes went around the nightclubs with his friends and colleagues, but he turned the pretty girls down when they asked him to take them home. During the week he concentrated on his work, often putting in many more hours than he had to. His surgery was in a restored colonial building a short way from the city centre. It was paid for by French money, and was as well equipped as any he had worked in at home. He saw a stream of children, most of them brought in from the countryside, with dental problems ranging from the mundane to the atrocious. Once he had become accustomed to the heat and found a few places go in the evenings to drink beer and play pool his life in Cambodia was almost ordinary, until the day a ten-year-old Malic walked into his surgery.

She looked terrified of all the shiny electrical equipment, her eyes darting from the chair to the drill to the stainless steel instruments all over the place. It was as though she were expecting them to explode at any moment, but there to reassure her was her elder sister. She spoke gently to the girl, and hugged her. Francois marvelled at the music of the young woman's voice, trembled at her grace and beauty and realised at once that he had not come to Cambodia to be kind to children or to enhance his CV, but had come for her, to collect her and to take her home. Together the sisters studied the young dentist, and talked about how kind he looked, and how handsome. Slowly Malic calmed down.

A small group of students stood around as her teeth were examined and photographed. It was a long process, and Francois couldn't help throwing occasional glances at Morakot, who had stayed in the room to reassure her sister. He tried to picture his fiancée being so kind and gentle with a child and, though he knew he was being irrational, he couldn't. After the examination he spoke to Morakot through his interpreter. He explained that although Malic's teeth were obviously in a very bad way, that they were in fact the most complicated set of teeth he had ever encountered, he and his colleague, a dentist with nearly thirty years experience, would do the best they could for her. As he spoke, Morakot looked with concern between him and her sister. He explained that he had other patients to see, but would be happy to meet the two of them for dinner that night, where he would be able to explain the necessary procedure at length. Morakot nodded, and arrangements were made.

It was Malic's first time in Phnom Penh. She had never seen so many motorbikes, cars, trucks and buses, not even on her trips to Battambang, and she found it strange to visit so many places she had seen on the television, like the King's palace, Wat Phnom with its bored-looking elephant, and the vast yellow dome of the Central Market, which looked as though it belonged in a cartoon. And there were foreigners everywhere. She had only ever seen a few of them before. Occasionally she and the other children had waved at them as they passed through her village on their motorbikes or in their jeeps. Once, a foreigner's motorbike had broken down near her home. Seeing her father's sign, the tall, red-faced man had wheeled it into the yard. Malic, Sophal and Panarith had watched from a distance as he sat, sweating, on an empty oil drum.

The restaurant where they met the dentist and his interpreter was full of foreigners and rich-looking Cambodians. Malic was mesmerised by her surroundings, and with her and Morakot in the new clothes they had been given for their trip she felt they had entered a different world. She hardly heard a word the others were saying as she gazed at the glass chandeliers and the big, bright picture of a waterfall that really seemed to be moving. The dentist had used up all his Khmer in minutes and had come to rely on his interpreter, a boy not much older than Morakot who had recently graduated from the university. When Malic did tune in to the conversation she noticed that they were talking about the weather in France, or what it was like to live in a Cambodian village. Malic thought it strange when Morakot agreed to meet the dentist again the following evening.

'It's very important,' she said, after they had

been driven back to the dormitory next door to the surgery. 'We have to talk about your teeth.'

When Malic's treatment began, she had to stay in the ward. So Morakot went out for meals with just the dentist and his interpreter, where they began to find out more about one another. He learned that she was twenty, and that her father had a natural talent for machines and could repair anything, that his business was doing well enough for him to be saving to send her to the city to train as a teacher. She told him that she was single, even though she had been approached by many boys, and that she spent her days reading borrowed books, and helping her parents around the house. She learned that the dentist lived somewhere to the north of Paris, that he had three sisters, and that he didn't have a girlfriend any more.

One evening, when Francois' interpreter had gone to Kampong Cham province to see his brother's new baby girl, they sat together in an expensive restaurant. When he was sure no one was looking he reached across the table and took her hand. She smiled. He kissed her in the taxi on the way back to the hospital where Malic lay, tormented by a nagging pain that everyone assured her was helping to make her better.

After five weeks of tests and photographs, Malic was told that she was ready to go home. As part of the treatment she had had three teeth removed, and she kept them wrapped in a piece of tissue paper. Francois had decided that it might not be ideal for the girl to make another trip to Phnom Penh for a while, so he should check up on her by visiting her at home. After all, she was his most extreme case. After getting detailed directions to their village he saw the sisters into the car that was going to take them home. They sat in the back, Malic with a mouth full of wires and a clamp around her head, and Morakot with a Walkman and a *Teach Yourself French* book and cassette pack. The driver played loud music for the whole nine hour journey, the same songs over and over again.

273

Francois watched the car until it had disappeared into the traffic, then went back to his apartment near the river.

Two weeks later the dentist arrived in their village, with his interpreter. He was dusty after the long ride, but declined to wash in the river. After spending a few hours with the girls' father, drinking Angkor beer and the cognac he had brought with him from the city, he fell asleep under a mosquito net in a neighbour's house.

In the morning he was exhausted and drenched with sweat after a torturous night without a fan. He spoke a little French with Morakot, who seemed self-conscious at her imitation of the voice on the cassette, told everyone that Malic's teeth were doing as well as could be expected, and set off back to Phnom Penh. Two weeks later he was back. Everyone in the village was pleased to see him again. They talked about how kind he was to Malic, how handsome he was, and how lucky Morakot would be if he asked her to marry him. Which he did, along the bank of the Mekong, when the girls were back in Phnom Penh to have Malic's teeth photographed for what they hoped would be the last time.

He had learned the words from his interpreter, who had assured him that she would say yes. He extended his contract for six months, and started sorting out the paperwork.

None of Francois' family came over for the wedding, but the room at the club was full of his drunken foreign friends. They made a big fuss of Malic, taking her around the miniature golf course and treating her to sweets and soft drinks. Some of them had Cambodian wives, and spoke Khmer clearly enough for her to understand some of what they were saying.

The couple lived in the dentist's apartment. Morakot took French lessons and cooked while her husband worked. In the evenings they played cards, and planned their move to France. He told her that before he started a new job he would take her around Europe for a few weeks, to see lots of famous places. He said he would take photographs of her everywhere they went, and that it would be cold and beautiful.

Morakot told Malic that she would think about her all the time, and that she would write to her as often as she could. Neither of their parents could read or write very well, so it would be Malic's job to tell them all her news, and to write back with any news of their own. Malic and her father went to the airport to say goodbye.

Sophal liked to reminisce about the adventures he had had with Panarith and his little sister Malic. He enjoyed telling stories about their trips along the river in his uncle's boat, and the times they wandered a long way from the village, out into the rice fields. The story he was asked to tell again and again was the one about the day when, finding a plastic water bottle floating in the river a little way from the village, they had tied the boat up and played football in a grove of coconut trees. Sophal bagged Cambodia before the others had thought to. Panarith was Arsenal, and his sister chose Laos. The teams kicked off, vying for possession of the bottle. Malic played fiercely for her adopted country. The goal, without a keeper, was between two tree trunks, and she was doing well. The score was Cambodia six, Laos four and Arsenal three when the bottle flew away from a hard tackle and landed a short distance away from the players. Arsenal and Laos raced towards it, and were so close that it seemed as though their bodies were fused as the ground exploded, throwing them into the air and spraying bits of their skin around the coconut grove.

Sophal screamed for help, but nobody came. He ran back to the river, and along the bank. He met two fishermen who had heard the noise and were coming to investigate. Together they ran to the scene. Only a few minutes had passed, but Panarith was already covered with big black ants. It must have been him who had trodden on the shell, as Sophal noticed that his friend's legs had been blown off somewhere around the middle of his thighs.

Sophal told anyone who cared to listen about how they made sure Panarith was dead, and left his body for later, how Malic was loaded, unconscious, first into the boat and then into the back of a truck, and how everybody said she was going to die before they reached a doctor. 'But she lived. She had half her face torn off by the explosion, though – her nose has gone and she lost most of her mouth. Now she has these holes in her face where they used to be.' He put two fingers from each hand into his mouth and pulled his lips back in imitation of Malic. 'Most of her teeth are gone, except a few here and there, and they are all over the place. She's been to Phnom Penh to have them fixed but it hasn't made much difference – she still can't talk properly. I can understand her some of the time, and so can her family, but people who don't know her can hardly work out a word she's saying because she hasn't really got any lips left, just these flaps of skin that don't meet up. She lost her left hand too. She's just got a stump, and she's got scars all over her chest. The doctors said they were surprised she didn't bleed to death, or die from an infection.

'The farmer couldn't work out how come he

or one of his animals hadn't exploded the shell long before. He said he must have walked over it a thousand times. If you want to see her she lives by that motorcycle repair place near the river. She's not a pretty sight though, I'm warning you. She's all . . .' He put his fingers in his mouth, and pulled his lips back in imitation of Malic.

Morakot wrote long letters to Malic at least once a week. Sometimes they took just three or four weeks to arrive, sometimes they took months, and sometimes they didn't arrive at all. They were sometimes delivered alone, sometimes in bundles, and almost always in the wrong order. Malic read and re-read them to herself, and told all Morakot's news to her mother, father and grandmother. Morakot told her sister so much about what it was like in France that Malic felt she could go there and not be surprised by anything. Each letter ended with Morakot saying how happy she was, how much she missed them, and that she and her husband would be visiting as soon as they could. The dentist had set up a bank account for her family, and the few American dollars he sent them every once in a while made them think he was very prosperous. Her father used the money to paint the stair rail and shutters blue, to replace the old wooden roof with corrugated iron, and to lay a concrete floor in his workshop. Malic always had nice sarongs to wear, and was given a motorbike of her own so she could run errands for her father. She replied to her sister's letters with news of the family and the village, and stories she had heard from further afield. She told her when their next-door neighbour, who was so deep in debt that she couldn't see a way out, had killed herself by drinking insecticide, and when the body of a seven-year-old girl from two villages away had been found face-down in an irrigation channel, having been raped, strangled and robbed of her gold earrings.

In one letter, Morakot told Malic that the dentist had said that when she was older he would pay for her to visit Europe, that he would take two weeks off work and take them both to Malic's favourite places in the photographs.

All of Malic's hopes for her future lay in her

village. While so many of the other children from her neighbourhood dreamed of moving to America or France, she wanted to stay near her mother and father, and the river and the muddy tracks she knew so well. Even so, she was overcome with excitement at the thought of, just once, stepping inside the photographs and standing in the places where her sister had stood. Morakot never mentioned the offer again, but Malic dreamed of the trip all the time. She imagined what the pictures would look like. When she returned home she would put them all together in an album, and on the front she would write, *Malic In Europe, Two Thousand And Whenever*.

When Morakot's letter arrived announcing her pregnancy, her father celebrated by drinking so much beer and palm wine that he had to be carried home. It took him three days to recover, and as soon as he could focus again he set about making a cart for his grandchild. Using various parts that were lying around his workshop, he worked in secrecy. Although word got out, he wouldn't let anybody see it until it was ready. Whenever he found a gap between paid jobs he got straight back to putting it together. When, after a fortnight, it was finally unveiled, people came by to have a look. They laughed at it, and admired it, having never seen anything like it before. Its body was made out of a reshaped truck door, and it had four bicycle wheels and a canvas hood to protect the baby's light skin from the sun.

People crowded around it, picturing the big, fat, half-French baby being paraded through the streets, propped up against the old Honda seat and seeing its mother's village for the first time. Once everyone had paid their respects to the cart, its proud inventor put it in the corner of his workshop and covered it in rags so it would be ready for when the baby came. He told Malic not to tell Morakot about it in her letters. It was to be a surprise.

Like everyone else, Malic proclaimed her excitement and joined in the speculation about the baby's name, and whether it would be a boy or a girl.

*   *   *

The baby was called Laetitia, and Morakot sent photographs of her. Malic spent hours looking at the baby's fat cheeks and brightly coloured clothes, and her tuft of light brown hair, and tried as hard as she could to be happy. She had never found anything so difficult. She missed the child so much she could hardly bear it. She wanted more than anything to carry Laetitia around the village, or wheel her around in the trolley, and have people come up and look at her and say how nice and fat she looked, and how happy. She wanted to scoop the little thing up in her arms and carry her to the river, where they would bob up and down in the water, and it would be her job to cover Laetitia's hair with soap and rinse it carefully so none of the bubbles went in her eyes. As they splashed around in the muddy brown water, the baby would look at her auntie Malic and smile as she was smiling in the photographs, her blue eyes bright with love.

Morakot wrote a letter saying that the dentist didn't want the baby to go to Cambodia until she was a lot older. She said he was worried about the germs.

*   *   *

Malic's favourite photograph was the one where her sister was standing in front of the lopsided tower in Italy. Sitting by her side, and looking longingly up at her was a scruffy dog. Morakot had told her all about how the dog had followed them from the street outside their guest house, and that he had seemed so nice and friendly that they hadn't wanted to chase him away. They had named him Henri, after one of the dentist's friends in Phnom Penh. The dog had stayed with them all day, and they had fed him biscuits and chocolate.

There were lots of scruffy dogs in Malic's village, but there was something about the one in the photograph that made him stick in her mind. She had often found herself imagining he was there by her side as she walked around, looking up at her adoringly with his beautiful eyes. She imagined he would still be there when she went to Italy, and that she too would feed him biscuits and chocolate.

But her daydreams about Henri were becoming less and less frequent. She had other things to daydream about now, like Laetitia and Sophal. Sometimes she found herself wondering what it would be like for Sophal to put his arms around her, to hold her so tight and kiss her so gently that it seemed her heart would burst with love.

As soon as the people who had been giving him snacks went back in to their guest house, the dog turned and headed straight back towards his home. By sunset he was in the countryside. Running and walking, and hunting, and finding and stealing food, he made his way east-south-east in as straight a line as he could, sometimes being chased and sometimes not, through gardens and farms, through towns and villages, along quiet and busy roads, through woods, around the edges of lakes, swimming across streams and rivers, and sometimes heading in the wrong direction for hours before finding the right way to go and turning back towards home.

In Pisa he had been further from his home than he had been in Rome, but he never stopped moving, except sometimes when he had been just too exhausted to go on and he had no choice but to hide away in the shade until he felt ready to pass along footpaths and along animal tracks and roads, having to run from people who didn't want him around, from sudden noises and from dogs who chased after him as he crossed their territory.

After a long time, as he neared his home, he started moving faster. Even though his feet were covered with cuts and his stomach was empty, his tail rose into the air and he stopped to eat and sleep a lot less.

Forty-nine days after leaving Pisa, a taxi drove past him as he made his way over fallen leaves along the side of a quiet road. It was carrying somebody who didn't notice him. The car's passenger was too busy trying to steal glimpses at the top of his own head in the rear view mirror, and tutting, and wondering where his youth had gone, and why it had gone so fast, like a nightfall that takes everybody by surprise. If he had noticed the dog he would have given him a ride, because they had met before. They were friends, and had the same destination in mind.

It's
true that I'm living
in a world flooded with
the light of Love—

TIMBO

A few months before Timoleon Vieta's arrival, Cockroft had bought a secondhand copy of *Madame Bovary* from an English language bookshop on a visit to Rome. Back at the house he had started to read it. He found it dull until, on page fifty-seven, Madame Bovary was given a greyhound. Suddenly the book came to life for him. The greyhound reminded him of the dogs he had owned, and when it bolted across the fields outside Yonville he had wept, recalling his own distress at the disappearance of his Samoyed. For the rest of the book he expected the dog to come back into its owner's life at any moment, to bound into the fair with its tongue hanging from the side of its mouth, to be waiting outside the opera house in Rouen and looking with its big greyhound eyes at Madame Bovary, or to lollop into the scene as its mistress lay dying with a belly full of arsenic, nuzzling her with its wet nose and giving her the strength to recover. Right up until the final line of the book, Cockroft had been expecting the dog to return. But, like the Samoyed, it never did.

Able to think of nothing but how much he missed Timoleon Vieta, he found the book on a shelf in the kitchen, and went back to the page where the greyhound had run away. He had put an asterisk where the passage began. He sniffed and fought back tears as he read the part where Monsieur Lheureux the draper had tried to console her with various instances of lost dogs having found their masters. Lheureux told of one travelling from Paris to Constantinople, and another which had gone a hundred and fifty miles in a straight line, swimming four rivers on the way. He even told her about his own father, whose poodle had, after twelve years away, suddenly jumped on his back in the street.

Cockroft knew them to be empty words of comfort. He had long since given up hope of the Samoyed ever returning, and he knew deep inside that he would never see Timoleon Vieta again, that his dog would never suddenly jump on his back in Assisi or Torgiano, or on the shores of Lake Trasimeno. He knew that he was never coming home.

The first thing that struck Cockroft as the boy from the photographs stepped out of the taxi, fumbling in his pockets for money, was that his fine, golden hair was almost all gone. It had thinned so much that from a distance he could almost have passed as an old man. Just a few strands clung to the top of his head. The second thing he noticed was just how little this mattered to him. The old man stood frozen, smiling like a baby.

'Hi,' said the boy, as the taxi drove away.

Cockroft couldn't move.

'Sorry about my hair.' He had thought about wearing a cap, but had decided to get the revelation over and done with as quickly as possible.

291

Cockroft tried to raise his eyebrows and casually shrug, but he couldn't.

'Erm, Cockroft?' The boy bit his lip. 'I know this is all out of the blue, but . . . would you mind if I stayed here and grew old with you? Can I? Would that be OK?'

Some air leaked out of Cockroft, making a high squeak.

'I mean if there's somebody else I'll just go.' He waved his hand dismissively. 'Really.'

The thought of him leaving snapped Cockroft into life. 'No,' he said. 'There's nobody else.'

'Really?' The boy tilted his bald head to one side, and narrowed his eyes. 'Cockroft?'

'No, really. There's no one.'

'What's his name?'

Cockroft sucked his lips and looked at the ground. 'I'm not sure.' He had never asked. He had wanted to, but the opportunity to raise the matter had long since passed. 'It's something really complicated. Bosnian. He's from Bosnia. I feel sorry for him, but I don't really like him. He's in the house right now. I'll ask him to go.'

'Does he love you? Will he fight me?'

Cockroft laughed, for the first time in months. 'No, he doesn't love me one little bit. He just . . .' He looked guilty.

'Just what?'

'Sucks my dick on Wednesdays.'

The boy looked at Cockroft, open-mouthed. 'That's like the infinite chimps,' he laughed. 'I can't believe that worked. You must have tried that ten thousand times. So there's something to be said for persistence after all. So if he doesn't love you he won't mind so much if I do this.' The boy smiled, walked up to Cockroft and threw his arms around him. 'It's so good to be home,' he said. He kissed the old man's lips, and played with his beard for a while.

'And how are Meshach, Shadrach and Abednego?'

'They're very well. They send their regards.'

'Do they?'

Cockroft looked at the ground. He loosened his grip on the boy. 'You know what I mean.' His grandchildren were three of the many things Cockroft spent all his time trying not to think about. He hadn't seen them for a long time. His son-in-law hated him, and blamed him for all the bad things that had happened, and wanted him to stay out of the children's lives. Christmas and birthday cards went unacknowledged, even when they were stuffed with lira for them to enjoy changing at Thomas Cook. Cockroft wasn't even sure of their address any more.

'I know what you mean,' said the boy, sadly. 'I'm sorry. I shouldn't have asked.'

'It's OK,' said Cockroft. They stood in silence.

'And where's my little Timbo?' the boy asked, smiling and looking around.

Cockroft had always winced whenever anyone had abbreviated Timoleon Vieta's name. Except this boy. He could get away with it. The old man sighed. 'He's gone. It's a long story. A long, sad, Cockroftian tale of drunkenness, misery and stupidity. I might as well have taken a gun to his head.' He looked into the distance. 'I'll tell you all about it later.'

'Can't I say anything right today?' The boy, seeing the agony in the old man's eyes, held him tight, and rubbed his nose around his beard.

After a while the boy said, 'I'm sorry about Misty.' He wanted to raise the subject straight away, so it wouldn't lurk in the background and drag them down. Once they had got all the awkward things out of the way they could start having fun again, and he wanted to start having fun as soon as possible. He meant what he said. He really was sorry for having run off with Monty 'Misty' Moore. 'It didn't last long. A year or two I suppose. I don't remember. Anyway I found somebody else after a while.'

Cockroft didn't say anything.

'You're right about him. I should have listened to you. He's an asshole.'

'I never said he was an asshole,' said Cockroft, abruptly, drawing back from the boy and putting his hands on his hips.

'What? How about all those stories about him stealing all your tunes and passing them off as his own? You had hundreds of them. You kept saying it was you who bought his swimming pool for him, and you who paid for all his weddings.'

'Well,' said Cockroft, gravely, 'no matter what I

may have accused that man of, I would never have called him an asshole.'

'Are you sure?'

'Absolutely. I've called him an *arse*hole more times than I can remember but I would never, in a million years, have called that man an *ass*hole. You Yankee dipshit.'

The boy smiled. 'I've missed you Cockroft,' he said, quietly, taking the old man's hands. 'You old cunt.'

The Bosnian, seeing this emotional reunion through the window, packed his things, and some of the old man's things, into his bag. He waited until the friends were in their bedroom, licking each other all over, before quietly leaving the house.

Timoleon Vieta turned off the main road and went up the track towards his master's house. He was exhausted and ravenous, but he moved quickly, almost like a young dog, his tail waving in the air.

*   *   *

The Bosnian walked down the track. He was going home. He told himself he couldn't live like this for another day, that he had to stop being frightened of the men who had shot him. He was tired of being frightened of them. He told himself that no matter how much he had wronged them they wouldn't be coming after him after such a long time, that they probably wouldn't even remember him, and that his fear was irrational.

His time away wouldn't really matter. Lots of people he knew had been around South America or India or Australia. He had been on a big journey too, only his had been a year and a half's travel through Italy. It wouldn't seem at all strange for him to have been out of the picture for a while. People would probably hardly even ask him about it, but if they did he would tell his family that he had been learning about life while walking in the footsteps of the poets, and tell his friends that he had been shacked up with a load of sultry signoras and naïve American girls, which wouldn't be too far from the truth. He wouldn't tell anybody about the long sleepless nights when he had avoided introspection by the width of a dog's whisker, or about the summer he had spent hiding penniless in the Umbrian hills with a lonely old man because he was scared stiff of being tracked down and killed by some rough people from Essex.

He thought about the people from Essex, about their faces, with their bad haircuts and their eyes that were too close together, about the way they had said things like *You're well out of your depth posh boy, my son,* and *We know where you live,* and *Wouldn't it be a shame if your dear old mother was to have a little . . . how shall I put it? . . . accident,* as though they were characters in a cheap television drama. At one point one of the men had even punched him hard in the face, raised his eyebrows, blown sarcastically on his knuckles and said *Whoops-a-daisy.* They were too small a set up to have had him followed, he told himself, just a load of chancers who probably shot people in the arm all the time and let the matter rest there having looked tough in front of one another and made their point. In fact, since the bullet had only grazed him, he wondered whether they had even meant to hit him at all. Maybe they had been too shocked to chase after him as he ran away, and were almost as scared as he was, able only to shout vague threats. Whatever, he felt sure he would be safe now. It wasn't as if he had set the police on to them or anything. He would go back to his family with his pack of lies, and find some cushy work in someone or other's firm. His father had wriggled out of his difficulties, keeping hold of his main house, which had exploded in value, and had built himself up again with the help of his old friends, who sorted him out with lucrative directorships here and there. A lot of money for occasionally sitting around and talking about tobacco, sandwiches or oil wells. It was almost as if nothing had happened, as if it had never seemed as though they had been on the verge of plummeting so catastrophically into the middle-middle classes. His mother had even mentioned the idea of buying another flat in London, and a place on the Algarve for golf. His father was sure to have lots of people who owed him favours by now, who would give a young man a well-paid position, and he would ask his friends to see what was available for him. He thought he could easily handle working in advertising, or in one of those jobs in the City that he had heard about. He sometimes called friends back home who told him about bonuses that paid for boats and BMs, that he could easily do the jobs they were doing, that they could probably sort him out with one, and how right he was to have got out of his business when he did, that London was full of cheap cocaine and it was more or less legal so every other rat-faced seventeen-year-old was selling it. He had found himself becoming wildly jealous of their lifestyles. He had missed a year and a half of being obstreperous in exclusive restaurants and high-handed with the waiting staff, a year and a half of taking taxis everywhere and giving niggardly tips to the drivers. He wanted to get drunk on expensive and elaborate cocktails like his friends did, and he wanted to justify an enormous pay packet by saying that he deserved it because he had worked hard for it, even though all he really did was move other people's money around. He wanted to go to Cowes Week with a load of loudmouthed yachties, and buy his cocaine from somebody else for a change. He wanted to fuck girls with big noses and thousand dollar hats. And suddenly he wanted his mother to call him Simon.

In his last call home, from a pay phone in Perugia, his mother had told him that his grandmother had not been well, and that it was only a matter of time. That would be his excuse for going home. It would make him look compassionate. He thought about buying a car and a flat with all the money, or at least renting a nice place by the river. He was jolted from his daydream by the sight of the dog that he and the old man had dumped in Rome coming up the track towards him. For a moment he couldn't believe what he was seeing.

Timoleon Vieta skulked over to the side of the track, his tail between his legs. The Bosnian laughed without smiling. He walked over to the exhausted dog, lunged and grabbed him by the scrawny scruff of his neck and lifted him up. The dog's back legs dangled a few inches off the ground. He was skinny, weak, and light. His coat was filthy and in some places so thin that his skin showed through. Even though the dog was growling and struggling, he had little strength and the Bosnian held him firmly in his grip. His knuckles were white.

'I am from Bosnia,' the Bosnian said. Holding the wriggling mongrel at arm's length he dropped his bag to the ground and rummaged around for his knife. He found it, inside the old sock he used as a sheath. He held it to one side of the dog's throat, pressed the blade through his fur and into his skin, and drew it across with all his strength. Blood shot out of the slit and sprayed on to the Bosnian's t-shirt, hands and arms. The dog made a choking sound, twitched, and fell still. The Bosnian dropped Timoleon Vieta on to the ground. 'I am from Bosnia,' he said, kicking and stamping on the dog's head and neck. 'I kill the dogs.' He felt Timoleon Vieta's skull give under the force of his boots. 'It is my instinct.' He kicked him into the middle of the track.

The dog lay dead on its side, one of its eyes facing upwards as though it could see the sky.

Noticing this, the Bosnian jabbed his knife into the eyeball over and over again, until it was a mess and no longer looked as though it could see the sky. He changed his t-shirt, wiping the blood from his hands and arms with his old one, and walked on down the track.

'I am called Simon,' he said. 'Simon.' His voice grew louder. 'My name is Simon,' he bellowed. 'Simon,' he shouted.

He reached the main road and walked towards the bus station, patting the bulge in his back pocket that was the old man's wad of lira, and leaving the Bosnian standing sentry over the body of the dog.

'Let's walk into town,' said the naked boy, who had left his silver shorts behind at an old man's house a long time before. They didn't go with a hopelessly receding hairline. He had found that there wasn't much that went with a hopelessly receding hairline. Old men had started paying him less and less attention. They wanted boys with hair. It was a tragedy. He had started spending time with people his own age, and although they were better than nothing he just couldn't get really excited by them. The main problem with them was that they just weren't old enough.

'It isn't summer any more, so let's walk there like we used to.' Peeping through the curtains of Cockroft's window they had watched the Bosnian leave with his bag over his shoulder, and had calculated that he would be long gone.

In the old days, when the weather was cool enough, they had played a game, seeing if they could hold hands all the way from the house down to the main road. If they thought they heard somebody coming they would disentangle their fingers and fall into the uncle-and-nephew routine that is such a common sight in Umbria, Tuscany and the Marches. The track was quiet, so they usually won the game.

'OK,' said the naked old man. 'But we're getting a taxi back. I'm not as young as I used to be, you know.'

'I know. That's what I like about you. You keep on getting older.'

They got dressed, locked up the house and joined hands. 'If only Timoleon Vieta were here,' sighed Cockroft.

The boy gave the old man's hand a squeeze, and thought of a way to cheer him up. 'Why is it that birds suddenly appear?' he asked.

'What? You mean every time I am in the general vicinity?' Cockroft smiled. 'Well I suppose the only logical explanation is that, in a similar way to you, they must long to be in my, well, general vicinity.' For some reason it had been their song.

They started it from the top and walked on down the track, swinging their arms and laughing at forgotten lines.

WWW.CANONGATE.NET

ONLINE READING *THAT* MATTERS

Click your way to Canongate's website for an almighty stash of book news, extracts, downloads, reading guides and shelves of literary goodies.

Plus, when you subscribe as a member we'll send you a free membership pack, regular news emails and a free book with every order.

"At last a publisher's website that feels like a cool club stocked with well-read friends rather than a lazy corporate exercise." [Guardian]